Magic Puppy

Books 1–3

SUE BENTLEY

Illustrated by Angela Swan

Grosset & Dunlap
An Imprint of Penguin Group (USA) LLC

Magic Puppy

A New Beginning

Puppy

SUE BENTLEY

To Cindy—first and best-beloved,

who was happy in a doll's pram.

GROSSET & DUNLAP
Published by the Penguin Group
Penguin Group (USA) LLC, 375 Hudson Street, New York, New York 10014, USA

USA | Canada | UK | Ireland | Australia | New Zealand | India | South Africa | China

penguin.com
A Penguin Random House Company

Text copyright © 2008 by Sue Bentley. Illustrations copyright © 2008 by Angela Swan. Cover illustrations copyright © 2008 by Andrew Farley. *A New Beginning*, *Muddy Paws*, and *Cloud Capers* first published in Great Britain in 2008 by Penguin Books Ltd, and in the United States in 2009 by Grosset & Dunlap. This bind-up edition first published in the United States in 2014 by Grosset & Dunlap, a division of Penguin Young Readers Group, 345 Hudson Street, New York, New York 10014. GROSSET & DUNLAP is a trademark of Penguin Group (USA) LLC. Printed in the USA.

The Library of Congress has cataloged the individual books under the following Control Numbers: 2008040076, 2008040078, 2008040077.

ISBN 978-0-448-48460-0   10 9 8 7 6 5 4 3 2 1

A New Beginning

SUE BENTLEY

Illustrated by Angela Swan

Grosset & Dunlap
An Imprint of Penguin Group (USA) LLC

Prologue

Storm whimpered as he crawled into the cave. Behind the young silver-gray wolf, stars glimmered in the purple sky.

Suddenly, a piercing howl echoed in the night air.

"Shadow!" Storm gasped, trembling with fear.

The fierce lone wolf who had attacked Storm and the Moon-claw pack was close by. Storm knew he had to disguise himself, and quickly!

There was a dazzling gold flash and a fountain of golden sparks that lit up the back of the cave for a brief second. Where the wolf cub had just stood, there now crouched a tiny, sandy golden retriever puppy with floppy ears and twinkling midnight-blue eyes.

Storm's little puppy heart beat fast. In that split second of light, he had seen his mother, the she-wolf, lying crumpled against a rock.

"Mother?" he whined, plunging deeper into the cave.

"Storm?" Canista lifted her head to answer him in a velvety growl.

In the dim light Storm could see his mother's heaving sides and hear her rapid breathing. He felt a new surge of panic. "You are hurt! Did Shadow attack you, too?"

Canista nodded weakly. "His bite is poisoned. It drains my strength."

Storm's blue eyes flared with sorrow and anger. "Shadow has already killed my father and my three litter brothers. I will face Shadow and fight him!"

"Bravely said, my son. But now is not the time. You are the only cub left of our Moon-claw pack. Go to the other world. Use this puppy disguise to hide. Return when your magic is stronger. Then, together, we will fight Shadow." Canista's head flopped back tiredly as she finished speaking.

Storm bowed his head. He did not want to leave her, but he knew his mother was right.

The sound of mighty paws and a thunderous snarl echoed from the mouth of the cave.

"Go, Storm. Save yourself," Canista growled urgently.

Storm's sandy fur ignited with gold sparks. He whined softly as he felt the power building inside him. The golden light around him grew brighter. And brighter . . .

Chapter

ONE

Lily Benson felt a leap of excitement as her dad pulled up outside Greengates riding stables.

"Yay! I love Saturday afternoons. I get to spend hours and hours with ponies!" she cried, jumping out of the car.

Lily went around to the open window and bent down to kiss her dad's cheek.

Mr. Benson laughed. "Careful you

don't get pony-overload!"

"There's no such thing," Lily said. Her bedroom walls were covered with posters of ponies, and her bookcase was crammed with riding books and magazines.

"What a shame. I was hoping you might stop bugging your mom and me to buy you one!" her dad said.

He was only joking, but Lily felt a pang. She was desperate for a pony of her own. But her parents were worried about the hard work and amount of time it would take to care for it. Lily knew they were hoping she'd be satisfied with having free rides in exchange for helping out at Greengates.

"I'll never stop asking in a zillion years. Ponies rule, Dad!" she said.

"You've got a one-track mind, Lily

Benson. Have a good time. See you later," he called, steering away from the curb.

Lily sighed. She waved good-bye and then went into the stable yard.

The main stable buildings were built around two sides of a square. A large gate at one end led to the grazing field. Just beyond the field Lily could see the house where Janie Green, who ran Greengates, lived.

Janie was outside the tack room with Treacle and Taffy, two of the smaller ponies. Two young children in riding gear stood waiting, ready to mount.

Janie looked up and smiled warmly as Lily approached. She had a round pretty face with twinkling brown eyes and was always cheerful. "Hi, Lily. I hope you're feeling energetic. We're fully booked this afternoon."

"Hi, Janie," Lily said. She patted Taffy's neck and stroked Treacle's nose. "What do you want me to do first?"

"You could give Don a hand with the cleaning, if you don't mind. He's over at Bandit's stall," Janie said.

"Okay," Lily said happily. Bandit was her favorite pony. She was a sweet-natured palomino with a golden-tan coat and a pale mane and tail. Lily would have loved to own a pony just like her.

As Lily went off to find the stable boy she saw even more young riders arriving with their parents. It looked like it was going to be a hectic afternoon.

Lily said hello to Bandit for a few minutes, before spending the next hour or so forking up droppings, wheeling them over to the pile, and spreading fresh bedding.

Riders and ponies came and went. Lily lent a hand where it was needed. It was a hot day, and she was soon red-faced and sweaty.

"Why don't you take a break and go and get a drink?" Don suggested as she helped him fill the hay nets and water buckets. He was tall and wiry, with dark-red hair, freckles, and a thin face.

"Phew! I think I will," Lily said, pushing a strand of damp blond hair back from her forehead.

She went to the stable's kitchen and had a long, cold drink of orange juice.

As Lily was walking back past the grazing fields, she noticed some trash blowing around on the grass and went to pick it up.

"Thanks, Lily. You're doing a great job!" Janie Green called, pausing to rest the heavy saddle she was carrying on the fence.

"It makes me so mad when people

leave stuff behind. Don't they care that a plastic bag could kill a pony if it eats it?" Lily said indignantly.

"I don't think they give it a thought. Maybe they'd be more careful if they did—but not everyone's into horses."

Lily shrugged. "That's their loss, then!"

"I'm with you on that!" Janie said, smiling. "Have you persuaded your parents to buy you a pony yet?"

Lily made a face, thinking miserably of the earlier conversation with her dad.

"I take it that's a sore point," Janie said.

Lily nodded. "I still have to convince them that I can fit taking care of a pony around my schoolwork. Mom and Dad think it would be too much for me and I should wait until I'm older."

"They might be right, you know,"

Janie said gently. "Looking after a pony
is a big commitment, and there are no
days off."

Lily felt her spirits sink. She thought
Janie would be on her side!

"Do you want to take Bandit out? We
just got a cancellation, so she's free for a
couple of hours," Janie said.

Lily brightened immediately at the
thought of a longer free ride than usual.
"Really? I can take her out by myself?"
she asked delightedly.

Janie nodded. "You've ridden her
plenty of times, and she's used to you. You
can take her along the bridle paths, but
don't go beyond the woods. Okay?"

Lily nodded, feeling proud that
Janie trusted her. "Thanks, Janie! That's
awesome!"

She dashed straight across to Bandit, who was already tacked up. "Hello, girl. We're going for a ride," she crooned, stroking the pony's nose.

Bandit gave a friendly neigh and nuzzled Lily's palm. Lily buckled on her riding hat before mounting the palomino pony and using her heels to nudge her forward.

They trotted out of Greengates and turned onto the bridle path that ran down the edge of a field. The path branched farther on and Lily took the way to the woods.

Other riders from the stables passed her on their way back.

As she and Bandit entered the shade of the trees, Lily's mind drifted into a wonderful daydream. It was easy to

imagine that Bandit was her own pony
and they were alone. The sound of other
riders was muffled, and she was screened
from them by the thick bushes. Sunlight
filtered through the leaves and speckled
everything with spots of light.

"I wish you were mine," Lily said
dreamily, leaning forward to pat Bandit's
satiny neck.

Suddenly Bandit stumbled on a tree root, and the reins were jerked right out of Lily's hands.

"Oh!" Lily pitched forward and fell right over the pony's neck. As the ground rushed up to meet her she closed her eyes, ready for the painful landing.

Chapter
TWO

The collision with the ground never came.

With a dazzling golden flash and a crackle of sparks, Lily found herself jerking to a sudden halt. Her eyes flew open in shock and she saw that she was caught inside a huge glowing golden net, in midair, half a foot above the ground!

Very slowly, Lily felt herself float down and land gently on some leaves. With a fizzing noise, the glowing net broke up into golden sparks and then melted away into the leaves.

Lily sat up, blinking confusedly. Her first thought was for Bandit. She whipped around and was relieved to see the pony nibbling some grass in a small clearing a few feet away.

"Your riding creature is fine. I hope that you are not injured," said a strange voice.

Lily stiffened. "W-who said that?"

A tiny puppy with sandy fur, floppy ears, and huge midnight-blue eyes crawled out from beneath a pile of leaves. "I did. My name is Storm of the Moon-claw pack. What are you? And what is the name of your pack?" it woofed.

Lily's jaw dropped as she stared at the puppy in utter amazement. She felt like pinching herself to make sure she wasn't dreaming. But she saw that the puppy was looking at her quizzically as if waiting for her to respond.

"I'm a g-girl. A human . . . I'm L-Lily. Lily Benson," she found herself stammering. "But I don't know what you mean about a pack."

"A human? I have heard of these." Storm's silky forehead wrinkled in a frown. Lily saw that he was beginning to tremble. "Can I trust you, Lily? I come from far away and I need your help."

Lily was still having difficulty taking this in, but she didn't want to frighten this amazing puppy away. He was absolutely gorgeous with the brightest midnight-blue eyes she had ever seen and big soft paws that looked too big for his body.

Very slowly she got up onto her knees and reached out her hand.

To Lily's delight, Storm edged closer and brushed her fingers with his damp little nose. His tail wagged nervously. Despite being so scared, the tiny puppy seemed to trust her.

"Why do you need my help?" she
asked gently.

Storm's deep-blue eyes flashed with
anger and sadness. "A lone wolf called
Shadow attacked us. My father and
brothers were killed and my mother is sick
and in hiding. Shadow wants to lead the
Moon-claw wolf pack, but the others will
not follow him as long as I am alive."

"Wolf pack? But you're a pup—" Lily
stopped as Storm held up a velvety sandy
paw and began backing away.

There was another dazzling bright
flash and a burst of gold sparks showered
over Lily, crackling around her feet on the
ground.

"Oh!" Lily rubbed her eyes, blinded
for a second. When she could see again,

she saw that the tiny sandy puppy was
gone. In its place now stood a majestic
young wolf with thick silver-gray fur and
glowing midnight-blue eyes.

"Storm?" Lily gasped, eyeing the
wolf's large teeth and thick neck-ruff that
glimmered with hundreds of gold sparks
like tiny yellow diamonds.

"Yes, Lily, it is me," Storm said in a
deep velvety growl.

Before Lily could get used to seeing

Storm as his magnificent real self, there
was a final gold flash and he appeared
once again as a cute sandy puppy.

"Wow! You really are a wolf. That's
an awesome disguise," she said, getting up
from her knees.

Storm began trembling again. "Not if
Shadow's magic finds me. Will you help
me hide?"

Lily's heart went out to the helpless
puppy. "Of course I will. You can live with
. . ." She trailed off as she remembered her
parents' rules about having no house pets.
They'd probably insist on taking Storm
to the pet care center. There must be
some way she could help the tiny puppy.
"Maybe I could smuggle you into my
house, but I don't see how I can hide you
for long," she said thoughtfully.

"Do not worry. I will use my magic so that only you will be able to see and hear me," Storm woofed.

"You can make yourself invisible? Wow!" Lily breathed. "No problem, then. You're coming home with me. Just let me catch Bandit. By the time we get back to Greengates, it'll be time for Dad to pick me up."

A few minutes later, as she cradled Storm in her lap on Bandit's back, a big smile spread across Lily's face. Never in her wildest dreams had she imagined having a magic puppy for a friend!

Chapter
THREE

"You should sleep in here in case
Mom or Dad gets suspicious," Lily told
Storm, spreading an old coat in the
bottom of her closet. "But when no one's
around, you can get on my bed."

Storm looked in the closet and then
padded around her bedroom, sniffing
everything and exploring. "This is a good
place."

"Glad you like it!" Lily said, beaming at him. "Are you hungry?"

The tiny puppy barked eagerly.

"Okay. I'll go and raid the kitchen to see what I can find. I won't be long."

Lily dashed downstairs. Luckily her dad was in the garden cutting the lawn and her mom had just gone out to her yoga class. She found some leftover chicken in the fridge and quickly broke a piece off for Storm.

Back upstairs, she watched as Storm ate hungrily and then sat back licking his lips. "That was delicious. I like human food."

"I'll get you some dog food later," Lily said.

Storm nodded. "Good. We will go hunting together!"

"I couldn't do that!" Lily said, horrified. "Anyway, there's no need. The store at the end of the street sells dog food in cans. I'll buy some with my allowance," she told him.

Storm yawned, showing his sharp little teeth. "I think that I will rest now." Padding over to the closet, he curled up on the old coat with a contented sigh and promptly went to sleep.

Lily watched the tiny puppy's furry sides

rising and falling. Almost immediately his paws twitched as he started dreaming. *He must be exhausted from his long journey*, she thought.

Leaving Storm to sleep, Lily reached for a book of pony stories and stretched out on her bed to read.

The book was really good and she hardly noticed time passing. She was halfway through an exciting story about a pony being stolen, when something leaped onto her bed and launched itself on top of her.

Lily almost jumped out of her skin. "Storm! You scared me!" she said, laughing as she rolled over onto her back. "Did you have a good nap?"

"Yes, thank you. I feel safe here with you," Storm woofed happily. Plonking his big soft paws on her book, he leaned up and began licking her chin.

Lily wrapped her arms around his plump little sandy body and gave him a cuddle. After a couple of minutes, Storm squirmed free and sprang onto the rug with a surprisingly loud thud for a tiny puppy.

"I would like to go outside now!"

"Okay," Lily said, getting up off the bed. "Our garden's not very big, but there's a field nearby. I'll take you for a walk over there."

Storm gave an eager little bark and followed her downstairs.

As they reached the hall, her dad appeared at the living room door. He had a frown on his face. "What was all that thumping upstairs? It sounded like a herd of elephants."

"Dad! I . . . er . . . thought you were outside," Lily gasped in panic.

She quickly shifted around, trying to stand in front of Storm, before she suddenly remembered that he was invisible. Then, realizing how strange that must look, she began bending and stretching her arms. "Whew! Whew!"

she puffed for added emphasis. "Just doing
some exercise. I'm trying to get in shape.
I was about to come and tell you that I'm
going out for a jog around the field!"

Her dad raised his eyebrows as Lily did
a jumping jack. "Well, I guess that's a good
idea. Maybe I'll come with you. I could
use some exercise, too."

"No!" Lily said hastily. "Someone . . .

um . . . from school might see me. I'll look like a real baby if I'm trailing around after you."

"Excuse me for trying to cramp your style," her dad joked. "What's brought this new fitness fad on?"

"I want to be ready for when I get my own pony! It's going to be hard work looking after it," Lily replied.

Her dad rolled his eyes. "I should have known what was at the bottom of this! Do you ever think of anything else besides ponies?"

"Nope! Well, actually, yes! But you wouldn't believe me if I told you!" Lily said, glancing at Storm, who was waiting by the front door. She jogged toward him before her dad could ask any more awkward questions. "See you later!"

Chapter
FOUR

As Lily put her school books into
her bag on Monday morning, Storm sat
watching her.

She smiled at him. "I love having you
living here with me, but I have to go out
for a few hours. Try not to get bored and
chew my rug or anything, or Mom will
freak!"

"I will not do anything like that,"

Storm yapped indignantly.

"Sorry. Sometimes I forget you're not an ordinary puppy," Lily said, bending down to pet his silky ears. "It's a shame there was only time for a quick walk around the field before breakfast. I'll take you out for a really long walk when I get back from school. Promise."

Storm looked up at her curiously. "What is school?"

"It's a place where kids go to learn. Teachers tell us stuff and give us homework to do, and we do projects and all kinds of things," Lily explained.

"School sounds interesting. I will come with you," Storm decided.

Lily grinned. "I wish you could, but pets aren't allowed . . ." She paused as she had a second thought. "Hey! Maybe you *can* come if you stay invisible! But you'd have to be really quiet and stay close to me. Mr. Poke, our class teacher, is very strict."

Storm's face brightened, and his little sandy tail started wagging with excitement. "I will make sure that no one will know I'm there—except you, Lily!"

"Cool! Let's go!" Lily put her backpack on the floor and opened it up.

"It might be best if you got inside. I have to cross some busy roads."

Storm jumped into her bag and settled next to her books and gym clothes. Lily put on her bag, said good-bye to her parents, and headed out of the front door.

"We'll probably meet Freema and Katy, my friends from class, on the way. I can't wait to see their faces when I tell them about you!" she said to Storm.

There was a scuffling noise from her bag. Storm popped his head out, his big dewy eyes looking into Lily's. "You cannot tell anyone my secret. Promise me, Lily," he woofed seriously.

Lily was disappointed. She had always wanted a pet to tell her friends about, especially a pony, but she had been really excited at the thought that she might be able to share her amazing magic puppy friend. She'd do anything if it would help keep Storm safe, though. "Okay, I promise. Cross my heart and hope to die," she said.

Storm nodded, satisfied.

As Lily and Storm reached the school gate, they saw Freema and Katy. There was another girl with them whom Lily hadn't seen before.

"Hi, Katy. Hi, Freema," Lily greeted her friends.

"Hi, Lily. This is my cousin, Adjoa," Freema explained. "She just moved here and is going to be in our class."

Adjoa was tall with shiny black hair, an oval face, and big brown eyes, just like Freema.

Lily smiled at her. "Welcome to our school, Adjoa."

"Thanks," Adjoa said shyly.

"Did you help out at Greengates this weekend?" Katy asked Lily as they walked into the school grounds.

Lily nodded. "It was great. I had an extra-long ride on Bandit. Janie let me take her up to the woods by myself."

"Cool!" Katy said.

"Do you like riding?" Adjoa asked Lily.

"It's my favorite thing in the whole world!" Lily replied. "How about you?"

"Adjoa loves ponies, too!" Freema said. She nudged her cousin. "Tell Lily about your pony."

Lily's eyes widened. "You've got your own pony? You're so lucky! What's its name?"

"Pixie. She's gorgeous and I love her to pieces," Adjoa said. "You can come over

one night after school and meet her if you
like."

"Thanks. I'd love to," Lily said,
beaming.

In the classroom, Lily took her usual
seat next to Katy. She put her bag on the
floor, so that Storm could jump out.

Storm gave himself a shake and then
trotted off to sniff around the room.

Mr. Poke took attendance. "And just
before we begin," he said, looking up, "I'd
like to welcome Adjoa Hardiker to the
class."

Adjoa smiled shyly as everyone
clapped, including Lily.

A few minutes later, Lily was leaning
over to watch Storm. She smiled to herself
as the tiny puppy weaved in and out of

the desks, his sandy tail wagging.

A voice called out, but Lily was engrossed by Storm's cute antics.

"Lily Benson, can you stop daydreaming and take out your history book, please?" the teacher's sarcastic voice said. Mr. Poke had a bald head with a fuzzy rim of hair around his ears. He had a way of looking down his nose when he was annoyed.

Lily's head snapped up. "Sorry, sir."

"Looks like old Poker Face got out of bed on the wrong side—again," Katy commented. Adjoa and Freema, who sat nearby, giggled.

Lily turned around and grinned at them.

"Okay, class. I'd like you to begin work on your projects, please. Quietly, if possible!" Mr. Poke ordered.

They were doing the Tudors. Lily was making a collage of Queen Elizabeth I. "I think I'll do her lace ruffle today. I need to get some pieces of paper and stuff from the art cabinet," she said to Katy, who was bent over writing in her notebook.

"Can we have a little more work and a little less talking, Lily Benson?" Mr. Poke drawled.

"Yes, sir." Lily felt herself turning pink as she got up and went to the cabinet. *I wasn't even doing anything*, she thought.

Storm padded over to her. "Are you all right, Lily? You look hot," he woofed.

"I'm fine. Not like *some* people," Lily murmured, glancing back at the grumpy teacher.

She pulled the cabinet's handle, but it

seemed to have gotten stuck. Grasping it more firmly, she pulled again, but the door still wouldn't budge.

"I will help," Storm yapped eagerly.

Lily saw Mr. Poke coming over with a frown on his face. "Uh-oh, you'd better be quick, Storm. Looks like Poker Face is on the war path," she whispered.

Lily felt an odd, warm tingling down her spine as gold sparks ignited in Storm's sandy coat, and the tips of his ears and tail fizzed with power. Something strange was going to happen.

Raising one big sandy front paw, Storm sent a shower of bright golden sparks whooshing toward the cabinet. With a faint crackle they sank into the wood. For a moment nothing happened and Lily thought Storm's magic hadn't worked.

"Out of the way, Lily. Let me do it," Mr. Poke said irritably, reaching the cabinet—just as the doors sprang open.

An explosion of papers, brushes, pens, and paints shot out. Mr. Poke flew backward as if he'd been blown by a wind machine and landed on the floor on his backside.

Rustle! Papers floated down around him.

Splat! A plastic jar of glue hit Mr. Poke on the chest, bursting and spreading all over his gray sweater.

Thwack! Brushes, pens, and pencils fell on him, sticking firmly to the glue.

The teacher sat there blinking in shock.

The whole class erupted in laughter. Katy, Adjoa, and Freema were helpless.

Lily tried hard to bite back the
laughter bubbling up inside her.

"Who packed the cabinet like that?"
Mr. Poke roared, his face bright red as he
scrambled to his feet. "I have to go and
get cleaned up. Keep working, class. I'll be
right back." He stomped off toward the
bathroom, pens and pencils falling with a

clatter as he walked away.

"I am sorry, Lily. I think I used too much magic," Storm woofed in dismay.

Making sure that no one was looking, Lily quickly patted him. "You did just fine. It serves Mr. Poke right!"

She began putting everything back into the cabinet. Katy, Freema, and Adjoa helped her. By the time Mr. Poke reappeared wearing a hideous orange, yellow, and brown striped T-shirt, the mess was all cleared up.

The rest of the morning passed quickly, and at lunchtime Lily shared her cheese sandwiches and chips with Storm. When they finished, she took him for a run across the fields. The excited puppy ran around, chasing leaves in the wind and tiring himself out. He spent the rest of the afternoon napping under Lily's chair.

After school, with Storm back in her bag, Lily walked home with her friends.

She paused at the end of her street. "Did you mean it about me coming over to see Pixie?" she asked Adjoa.

Adjoa nodded. "Why don't you come over after school on Friday? We can both ride Pixie."

"That would be awesome!" Lily said. She jotted Adjoa's address and phone number in her notebook before heading home. "Bye. See you all tomorrow!" she called.

Katy, Freema, and Adjoa waved as they walked away.

Just inside her front garden, Lily put her bag down so that Storm could jump

out. "Adjoa's nice, isn't she?" she said to
him. "I can't wait to meet Pixie."

"Me too!" Storm nodded, his pink
tongue hanging in a doggy grin.

Lily felt a surge of affection for him.
She picked Storm up and petted his soft
sandy fur. "Having you at school today
was awesome! You really taught old Poker
Face a lesson. I hope that horrible Shadow
never finds you and then you can live with
me forever and come to school every day,"
she said.

"That is not possible, Lily," Storm told her, his small sandy face suddenly serious. "One day I must return to my own world to help heal my mother and fight Shadow."

Lily knew this was true, but she didn't want to believe it. She pushed all thoughts of Storm having to leave out of her mind and thought instead of the fun they would have on Friday with Adjoa and Pixie.

Chapter
FIVE

"Here you are, girl." Lily held a piece of carrot on the palm of her hand, so that Pixie could take it with her soft lips. Pixie was a chestnut pony with a white line down her nose and a friendly expression.

Lily turned to Adjoa as the pony crunched the treat. "Pixie is gorgeous!"

Adjoa smiled. "I know. I'm lucky to have her."

Pixie whinnied softly and swiveled her ears.

"I think she agrees with you," Lily said. They both laughed.

Adjoa opened the field gate and Lily helped her saddle the pony, and then both girls spent a couple of hours taking turns riding her. Lily thought with a sigh how wonderful it would be to have her own pony and ride her every day.

Storm bounded alongside the pony at first as Lily trotted around the field on her, but his short legs soon got tired. Lily couldn't lift him onto her lap with Adjoa watching. "Are you okay? You're not getting bored?" she leaned down to whisper to him.

"I am fine. I will go and explore," Storm barked softly.

Lily watched him go frolicking off toward the open-sided, wooden shelter at the bottom of the field. She could see him sniffing all the interesting smells in patches of long grass on the way.

With Storm happily occupied, Lily went back to enjoying her ride. Afterward she helped Adjoa untack Pixie and then rub her down before letting her run free. The pony immediately threw herself onto her back and rolled around. Storm ran straight up to her barking happily.

"Oh no!" Lily gasped, only just stopping herself from calling out to warn Storm to be careful. If Pixie kicked, the tiny puppy could get badly hurt by her hooves.

"What's wrong?" Adjoa asked, frowning.

"Er . . . nothing," Lily murmured, watching tensely as Pixie got to her feet again and shook herself. Her ears flattened as she looked down at the playful puppy, then she leaned down and gently nudged Storm's sandy fur. Storm yapped delightedly, wagging his tail.

Lily gave a big sigh of relief, which she quickly turned into a cough. She turned to Adjoa. "Sorry. I . . . um . . . thought I saw a rat in the straw in Pixie's shelter!"

Adjoa shrugged. "That's no big deal. The farmer's cats will catch it. Let's go in the house and get a drink." She opened the field gate that led straight into her back garden.

"Okay. I'll follow you in a sec. I think I've got a stone in my boot." Bending down so that she had her back to Adjoa, Lily motioned to Storm.

Storm scampered straight over and squeezed under the fence into the back garden. He trotted at Lily's heel, panting happily as they all walked toward the house.

In the kitchen, Adjoa's mom was getting cold drinks from the fridge. "I saw you coming," she said, smiling. "You must be Lily. It's nice to meet you. I'm glad Adjoa's already made a new friend." Her rows of tiny black braids were pinned up into a bun. She wore gold hoop earrings, jeans, and a pretty green top.

"Thanks for the drink, Mrs Hardiker," Lily said politely.

After their drinks, Lily and Storm went up to Adjoa's room. "It's just like mine!" Lily said delightedly, looking at all the pony posters and books. Red and blue ribbons that Adjoa had won for her riding were pinned around her mirror.

"That was so much fun! Thanks," Lily said to Adjoa before she left for home.

"That's okay. You can come here anytime," Adjoa said, smiling. "See you at school on Monday!"

As she walked away with Storm, Lily was thoughtful. "Adjoa's mom and dad don't seem to have a problem with their daughter taking care of a pony and doing homework. But I don't think I'll *ever* persuade mine to let me have one," she said to him with a sigh.

Storm barked in sympathy, wagging his tail. His thick sandy fur gleamed with tiny golden sparks. "Maybe I can help you," he woofed softly.

The following afternoon, Mrs. Benson dropped Lily and Storm off early at Greengates before she went to her yoga workshop. Lily had been silently thinking about what Storm had said; now she was bursting to ask him about it.

"Did you mean it, about helping me to get my own pony?" she asked as they walked across the stable yard.

Storm looked at her with alert midnight-blue eyes. "I did, Lily. I always keep my promises."

Lily waited, but Storm didn't say

anything more. Her imagination went into
overdrive. "I bet you're going to use your
magic to make a pony appear out of thin
air, aren't you? Are you going to put Mom
and Dad into a trance or something, so
they let me keep it?" she asked excitedly.

Storm's furry brow dipped in a frown.
"No. That would not be the right thing to
do, Lily. I am afraid that you will have to
be patient," he woofed mysteriously. He
leaped forward and went off to explore
the yard, shedding a few tiny gold sparks,
which glinted in the bright sunlight
before dissolving.

Lily stared after Storm. She knew she
was going to have to do as he said, but it
was hard to be patient when you wanted
something so much.

It was time that she went to see what
jobs needed doing, but first Lily went
to visit Bandit. She had an apple in her
pocket for the pony.

But the palomino wasn't in her stable,
so Lily went to check the grazing field.
Bandit wasn't there either. As she was

walking back across the yard feeling puzzled, Don came out of the tack room holding a saddle.

"Is Bandit out on an early ride?" Lily asked the stable boy.

"No. Bandit's already gone. Didn't Janie tell you?" Don said.

"Gone? Gone where?" Lily asked.

"To her new home," Don explained. "Bandit's quite old now, and Janie's been thinking about retiring her for some time. Someone came by during the week and offered Bandit a new home on the spot. Janie jumped at it. Bandit went to live in a field with two goats and a donkey for company."

"Oh, she'll really love that," Lily said, trying hard not to feel sad. But she knew

she was really going to miss the gentle old
pony.

Don's freckled face crinkled in a smile.
"It's amazing that somewhere so perfect
came right out of the blue, when Janie
hadn't really started looking yet. Just like
magic, really. Anyway, see you later." He
went off to tack up a pony.

Storm came rushing across the yard,
with a dusty nose from where he'd been
searching around in some straw. He gave
her a wide doggy grin and flopped down
at her feet.

Lily looked down at him thoughtfully.
"Did you have anything to do with
finding Bandit a perfect new home, by any
chance?"

Storm gave her a sideways look. He

twitched his nose. "I smell rabbits!" he
yelped happily and shot off again toward
the grazing field.

Lily stared after him. He was up to
something, she was sure of it.

Chapter
SIX

It had been another busy afternoon at Greengates. Lily was hanging up a pile of newly cleaned bridles in the tack room.

Janie popped her head in the door. "Why don't you leave that and go have a ride? Tinka's still saddled up."

"Thanks, Janie!" Glancing over to where Storm was napping on top of the brush box, Lily called to him. "Come on, Storm."

Storm's head shot up immediately. He jumped down and padded after Lily to where Tinka was tied to the fence.

Lily buckled on her riding hat before mounting the handsome bay pony. She walked Tinka out of the yard and onto the bridle path. This time she took the fork leading to a field that the riding school had permission to use. Storm ran along beside her, his ears flapping as Lily rode down a tractor path.

Lily had to concentrate very hard when riding Tinka. The bay pony was less experienced than dear old Bandit had been. Lily dismounted and was opening the field gate, when a wood pigeon fluttered up out of a bush. Startled, Tinka threw up her head and danced sideways.

"It's okay, girl." Lily spoke reassuringly, petting Tinka's nose to calm her.

As Tinka backed up, Lily noticed a ditch almost concealed in the long grass by the hedge. Someone had dumped some sharp hawthorn branches in it. Luckily, Tinka had just missed it or she could have been injured. Lily made a mental note to tell Janie about the dangerous ditch when she got back to Greengates.

Storm sat in her lap as Lily continued her ride. But as she made her way back

an hour or so later he ran along beside
her again. She saw him run off into the
field and start jumping around, barking
at butterflies and sticking his nose in
molehills. By the time Lily got back to the
field gate and dismounted again, Storm
was behind her.

Lily led Tinka through and was closing
the gate, when she spotted a familiar pony
and rider coming toward her along the
edge of the field. "Look, Storm! It's Adjoa
on Pixie!" she cried delightedly.

A moist brown nose and then two
sandy ears appeared as Storm squeezed
through a small gap in the hedge. He gave
an excited bark and leaped toward the
long grass.

Lily realized that he was heading
straight for the concealed ditch. "Storm!

Look out!" she cried. But the puppy was so set on reaching his friend Pixie that he didn't hear her.

Lily threw herself forward. She missed Storm, but just managed to push him sideways as she lost her balance and slid into the ditch.

"Ow!" she gasped with pain as her

ankle twisted and sharp thorns dug into
her leg.

Storm looked down at her in dismay.
"You saved me, Lily. But you are hurt. I
will help you," he whined.

"I . . . I think I'm okay," Lily said
shakily, biting back tears at the sharp ache
in her leg. Her riding pants were torn and
smeared with grass stains.

Time seemed to stand still. Lily felt
a familiar warm tingling down her back
as vivid gold sparks ignited in Storm's
fur. His tail stiffened and crackled with
power. Raising a velvety front paw Storm
sent a whoosh of sparks fizzing toward
Lily's injured leg. For a second the pain
increased and then it drained away just as
if someone had poured it down a drain.

When the bright sparks faded,

Lily saw that her riding pants were clean and fixed, too. "Thanks, Storm," she whispered.

"You are welcome," Storm woofed as the final gold sparks faded from his thick sandy fur.

Lily quickly climbed out of the ditch. She stood up as Adjoa pulled Pixie to a halt a couple of feet away. "Watch out for this ditch. You can hardly see it. I . . . er . . . nearly just slipped right into . . . ," she blustered. Lily racked her brain for an explanation that didn't involve Storm, but Adjoa wasn't listening.

Her new friend's eyes were red and puffy. It was obvious that Adjoa had been crying. Lily felt sad for her friend. What could be wrong?

Lily held Tinka by her reins and listened with growing dismay to what Adjoa had to say.

"The farmer who we rent Pixie's field from is selling it and we can't find another field nearby. Mom and Dad say it would cost too much to put her into stables where she'd be cared for, and so we might have to sell her," Adjoa said tearfully.

"Oh no! That's terrible," Lily exclaimed, putting one arm around her friend.

She knew it was expensive to have a

pony looked after by a stable. But it was awful to think of Adjoa losing her beloved pony.

Beside her Pixie gave a friendly blow and dipped her head to nuzzle Storm gently. The tiny puppy was lying on his back in the grass with all four legs in the air, showing his fat pale tummy. For once, Lily felt too upset for Adjoa to smile at his playful antics.

An idea came to her. She was going to talk to her parents.

Chapter
SEVEN

"I'm sorry, Lily. But my answer has to be the same," Mrs. Benson said.

They were all sitting in the kitchen on Saturday evening. Storm was lying down next to Lily's chair, invisible to everyone except her, as usual. Lily had just finished explaining about Pixie in the hope that her parents might be willing to buy the pony.

"I agree with your mom," Mr. Benson said. "Looking after a pony is a big responsibility. We're just not sure this is the right time for you to take that on."

"But it is, Dad! I'd be the best pony owner ever!" Lily said in her best pleading voice. "And if we bought Pixie, Adjoa could still see her whenever she wanted."

Her dad smiled and reached out to ruffle her hair. "I'm sorry, honey. I feel bad for Adjoa, too, but the subject's closed."

"That's what I thought you'd say," Lily said, sighing heavily.

All that evening and throughout Sunday, Adjoa and Pixie were on Lily's mind. On Monday, when she and Storm walked to school, they met up with Katy and Freema, but Adjoa wasn't with them.

"Where's Adjoa?" Lily asked.

"She's not coming in today. My aunt says she's got an upset tummy," Freema explained.

"I know *why* Adjoa's tummy is upset. It's because she's so worried about what's going to happen to Pixie," Lily said sadly.

Freema and Katy nodded.

When they reached the coatroom, Lily hung back and let her friends go into school ahead of her. "I wish I could think of a way to help Adjoa keep Pixie," she whispered to Storm. "But I've already tried Mom and Dad. I don't know what else I can do."

Storm whined softly in sympathy and
then his big midnight-blue eyes lit up.
"You could talk to the lady who runs the
riding stables," he suggested.

"Janie? I can't see what good that
would do," Lily said, frowning.

Storm barked encouragingly, wagging
his tail and dancing around her feet in
circles. Lily smiled. "Well, okay then, if
you're that sure it'll help. We'll stop over
there tonight after school. Uh-oh! Watch
out! Mr. Poke just came in. We'd better go
into class!" she hissed out of the side of
her mouth.

Back home after school, Lily quickly
changed into her jeans and T-shirt, before
running downstairs. She found her mom
in the kitchen. "Could you give me a ride
over to Greengates, please?" she asked.

Her mom looked surprised. "Don't
you get enough of that place on the
weekends? Why do you want to go over
there now?"

Lily thought quickly. "Tinka was sick

on Saturday. I wanted to check and see if she's any better," she lied.

Mrs. Benson smiled. "That's nice of you. You're a sweet person, Lily Benson."

Lily blushed, feeling a little guilty. But there was no way she could tell her mom that it was Storm's suggestion to go and talk to Janie. Anyway, it was true that she was always happy to see Tinka and all the other ponies. "So can I have a ride?" she asked.

Her mom nodded. "We'll go now. I have to go to the supermarket, so I can drop you off at Greengates and then pick you up on my way back."

Lily sat in the back of the car, with Storm on her lap as they drove there. She got out of the car at Greengates's main entrance. "Thanks for the ride, Mom.

I'll see you later."

As soon as her mom had driven away, Lily went into the yard. Storm trotted purposefully at her heels, invisible as usual.

She could see Janie sitting at her computer through the office window.

Lily paused, feeling uncertain. "Well, here I am. But I'm still not sure why! What am I supposed to say to her?" she whispered to Storm.

The puppy's luminous midnight-blue eyes looked even brighter than usual. "I think you should tell Janie about how Pixie needs a home," he woofed.

Lily frowned. "But there's no point. Greengates isn't a stable. It's a riding school. And anyway, Janie doesn't have room for any extra ponies. All the loose boxes are full."

Storm pricked his ears. "Not all of them."

Lily blinked as she realized what Storm was hinting at. "You're right! Bandit's not here anymore."

Storm nodded, looking very pleased with himself.

Before Lily could ask him anything else, Janie came out into the yard. "Lily? This is a nice surprise. What can I do for you?" she said.

"I . . . um . . ." Lily bit her lip, feeling

herself blushing as she struggled to find the right words to say. Now that she was here, her mind seemed to have gone completely blank.

Chapter
EIGHT

Storm gave a gentle woof, and as Lily looked down into his sparkling midnight-blue eyes, she felt herself starting to calm down.

Lily took a deep breath, and suddenly it all came pouring out. "I . . . um . . . wanted to ask you something. I've got a friend named Adjoa who's got a pony named Pixie. She's very sweet-natured, but

the farmer who owns her field is selling it.
And I thought, well, I was hoping—"

Janie smiled. "Whoa! Slow down a bit.
Let's go into my office, Lily. I could use a
break from working on my accounts. We'll
have a cold drink and you can tell me all
about it."

A few minutes later, Lily sat sipping
her apple juice as Janie tapped her fingers
on the desk thoughtfully.

"So what you're really asking is for
me to put Pixie into the stable?" she said
to Lily.

Lily nodded, feeling encouraged by
Janie's calmness and willingness to listen.
Everything seemed to have slotted into
place and become clear in her mind. Now
Lily knew exactly what to say.

"What about if Pixie lives here

and works as one of the riding school
ponies? Adjoa would have to agree, but
I think she'd do anything if it meant she
could keep Pixie. She'd still own her,
so she'd help look after her and pay for
Pixie's food and bedding and stuff. But it
probably wouldn't cost anywhere near as
much as a normal stable."

"You seem to have this all worked
out," Janie said.

"I do!" Lily said firmly.

"Hmm. It could work. We've had arrangements like this in the past and we are a pony short now that Bandit's gone. But I'd have to try Pixie out before I decided that she was right for Greengates. She'd have to be gentle, friendly, and dependable."

"Oh, she is! She's perfect. Should I ask Adjoa's parents to call you and set up a meeting?" Lily asked eagerly.

Janie nodded, smiling. "Yes. You're one determined young lady, Lily Benson."

"That's what my dad says!" Lily beamed at Janie as she got up. "Thanks so much, Janie. Is it okay if I go and see Tinka and the other ponies? I have just enough time before Mom picks me up."

"Of course it is. I'll leave you to it. I'd better get back to these accounts."

Lily and Storm spent twenty minutes
with the ponies before going back to
the riding stable's entrance. Mrs. Benson
had just arrived and was waiting to pick
her up.

On the way home in the back of the
car, Lily stroked Storm's floppy sandy ears.

"You had this all worked out, didn't you?" she said softly.

Storm nodded. "But I could not have done it all by myself. It was you who spoke to Janie. You did it, Lily."

Lily felt a warm glow of pride. It felt good to have helped her friend. "I can't wait to tell Adjoa all about it. I'm going to call her as soon as I get home."

The moment her mom pulled into the driveway, Lily shot out of the car and dashed toward the house.

"Er, excuse me, young lady! I could use some help with the groceries," her mom called after her.

"Sorry," Lily said sheepishly.

She rushed back, grabbed some bags, and dumped them on the kitchen table.

As she was coming out of the kitchen, the phone rang.

It was Adjoa's mom. "Hello, Lily. Is Adjoa with you? Can I have a word with her, please?" she asked.

"She isn't here," Lily replied, puzzled.

"Oh my, I was hoping she'd ridden Pixie over to see you," Mrs. Hardiker said, sounding worried. "Could I talk to your mom?"

Lily passed the phone over. "It's Adjoa's mom."

Lily waited impatiently while the two moms spoke. "What's going on?" she asked as her mom hung up the phone.

"Adjoa left a note saying she couldn't handle giving up Pixie, and some of her clothes are missing. Mrs. Hardiker was hoping she'd come over here. But it's beginning to look like Adjoa has run away with Pixie."

"Oh no!" Lily gasped.

Chapter
NINE

"It'll be dark soon. Adjoa must be so scared. We have to find her and tell her the news about Greengates!" Lily said to Storm as soon as they were alone in her bedroom.

Storm nodded. "I will take us to Adjoa's house and see if I can pick up a fresh trail."

Lily felt a familiar warm tingling down

her back as gold sparks crackled in Storm's sandy fur and a fountain of golden glitter streamed out of his tail. There was a bright flash and a whooshing sensation, and suddenly Lily found herself standing with Storm outside Pixie's field at the back of Adjoa's house.

Storm sniffed around, picking up Pixie's scent. Moments later, he stiffened. Lily saw that his moist brown nose was glowing like a gold nugget. "This way!" he barked, setting off at a run.

Lily followed Storm away from the field and through the streets. They hurried along the main road and then toward the edge of town. The street lights had already come on. Overhead the first stars had begun twinkling in the sky.

Lily grew hot and sweaty as she and

Storm followed Pixie's trail, but she wasn't tired. Gold sparks flashed past her as Storm's magic made them travel in double-quick time. Gradually Lily realized where they were heading.

"Greengates is just over there. Adjoa must have taken the bridle path. I bet she's planning to hide in the woods overnight. She'll probably take the shortcut across the fields," she told Storm.

A few minutes later, Storm barked and wagged his tail. "Over there!"

In the twilight, Lily could just make out the figure of a pony and rider against the shadowy bushes. The moon came out from behind a cloud and Lily could see more clearly. "It's them!" she cried.

Lily saw that Pixie was trotting toward the familiar field gate. "That ditch! Adjoa's heading straight for it. Those prickly branches have been cleared away since I told Janie about it, but a pony could still break her leg if she stumbles into it. I bet she's too upset to remember it's there, and Pixie won't see it in the dark!"

Storm's midnight-blue eyes flashed. Another rainbow of sparks shot out ahead of him and he leaped forward into the stream of light. Lily felt herself shooting

through the air beside him. She and Storm
landed a few feet in front of Adjoa and
Pixie.

Lily walked forward, holding up her
arms. "It's me, Lily! Adjoa, stop!"

Adjoa reined Pixie in. The pony's ears
swiveled and her head came up, but she
halted calmly a few paces away from the
ditch.

"Lily! What are you doing here? How
did you find me?" Adjoa cried.

"Don't worry about that now," Lily
said. "That ditch I fell into the other day
is right in front of you. Pixie could have
stumbled into it. Come over here. I have
to tell you something."

Adjoa urged Pixie over to one side,
but she didn't dismount. She looked
shaken, but determined. "Thanks for

reminding me about that ditch. But if you're going to try and persuade me to go back home, don't bother!" Adjoa said, looking down at Lily.

"Adjoa, listen! I've got some great news," Lily said quickly before her friend could decide to ride away. "I talked with Janie at Greengates. She's willing to take Pixie into her stable on the condition that you let her be used for the riding school."

"Really?" Adjoa looked stunned, but her hands loosened on the reins. Her shoulders relaxed as she thought about it. "I wouldn't mind little kids riding Pixie, and she'd enjoy the extra exercise. Dad said she was getting a bit fat anyway. But even with Janie using Pixie for rides, it's still going to cost a lot to keep her stabled at Greengates. I still don't know if Mom and Dad will agree."

Lily's face fell. She hadn't thought of this. It seemed as if there was a flaw in her awesome plan.

Storm jumped up with his paws on Lily's leg and woofed for attention. Lily looked down at him. "You could ask your mom and dad to help," he suggested in a soft bark.

It was a few seconds before Storm's words sank in. "That's it!" she burst out, her eyes widening.

"What is?" Adjoa said, puzzled.

"I just had a brilliant idea. Come on, Adjoa. We're going back to talk to my parents!" She quickly outlined her plan.

A look of hope came over Adjoa's face. "Do you think they'll agree?"

"They have to. It's Pixie's last chance," Lily said determinedly, turning on her heel, confident that Adjoa would now follow her on Pixie. At her side, Storm gave an encouraging yelp.

C h a p t e r
TEN

Later that evening, Lily sat at the kitchen table eating a pizza with her mom and dad. Storm was curled up under the table.

"You did a great job persuading Adjoa to come home," her dad said. "Her parents were almost out of their minds with worry. They've been on the phone saying how great you are. Good work, sweetie."

Lily felt herself blushing. "Anyone would have done the same."

"I'm not sure that's true," her mom said, patting her hand. "What I still can't figure out is how you found her so quickly and got up to the field near Greengates in record time."

"It must be all the exercise I've been doing. Mmm. This pizza's delish!" Lily said, quickly changing the subject. She slipped a small piece under the table for Storm to munch. "Mo-om? Da-ad?" she said in a persuading voice. "I've . . . um . . . got something to ask you."

Her parents exchanged glances. "I hope this isn't about having your own pony again!" Mrs. Benson said.

"Of course it's not," Lily said brightly.

"Thank goodness for that!" her dad said.

Lily paused for effect. "It's about me having half a pony!"

Mr. Benson frowned. "Run that by me again."

Lily grinned. "What I really mean is *sharing* a pony!" She explained about Janie agreeing to take Pixie into the stable and being a riding school pony. "But it's still going to be very expensive, so Adjoa's parents might decide to sell Pixie anyway. But they won't if we help with the costs.

And then I'd be sort of sharing a pony
with Adjoa. I'd be able to groom Pixie and
ride her sometimes. What do you think?"

"I think Pixie's going to be one busy
pony!" her dad said, smiling. "But it's an
interesting idea."

Lily held her breath and had all her
fingers and toes crossed. At least her dad
hadn't said no right away like he usually
did.

"I know you, Lily. You'll want to be
up at Greengates every night, looking
after Pixie and grooming her," said Mrs.
Benson. "I'm still worried that your
schoolwork could suffer."

"I know I might want to do that, but
I won't, because I'll know that I have to
take turns with Adjoa," Lily said honestly.
"I'll just be so happy to be able to ride

Pixie sometimes—and pretend she's all mine until I get a pony of my own one day!"

Her mom and dad exchanged glances.

"Well, when you put it like that, it sounds like a fair arrangement," her mom said.

"And it's the only way Lily's ever going to give us any peace! So the answer's yes," her dad added.

"Yay!" Lily flung herself at her parents and gave them both huge hugs and then did a little dance around the table. "I can't wait to tell Adjoa!"

Storm ran out from under the table and jumped up and down, barking excitedly. Lily grinned and just barely managed to stop herself from bending down and picking him up.

Later that night, Lily closed her
bedroom curtains, getting ready for bed.
Outside in the street she saw a
couple of people taking their dogs for a

walk. She jumped into bed and snuggled up under the blankets with Storm.

"Thanks so much for everything, Storm. You kept your promise about helping me get a pony, even though things turned out differently than how I imagined! You're the most awesome friend ever. We're going to have an amazing summer with Pixie and Adjoa!"

Storm tucked his head under her chin. "I am glad I was able to help."

Suddenly Lily heard howling and growling from outside in the street. She jumped back out of bed and peered through the bedroom curtains. The two dog walkers were struggling to control their dogs, which were pulling at their leashes and looking up at her bedroom. In the light of the streetlamps, the dogs' eyes looked pale and were glowing.

"That's weird . . ." Lily said, turning to Storm.

The tiny puppy was hiding in the bed. She could see him trembling with fright.

Frowning, Lily glanced outside again and saw the dogs suddenly calm down. After a moment, their confused owners walked on until they were out of sight.

Lily came back to Storm. As she went to pet him she realized that he was still shaking all over. "What's wrong? Are you sick?" she asked worriedly.

Storm shook his head. His ears were laid back and his tail was tucked beneath him. "I sense that Shadow is close. I think he used his magic, so that the dogs outside would attack me."

Lily looked at her friend in dismay. "Is that what he'll do if he finds you?"

Storm nodded, his eyes as dull as blue stones. "All the dogs around here will be looking for me now. I will use my magic to mask my scent. It may give me a little more time."

Lily kissed the top of his sandy head, breathing in his sweet puppy smell, and lay awake, hoping that Storm would be safe. She didn't think she could bear it if she never saw him again.

Chapter
ELEVEN

Lily woke up with a start the next morning. To her relief, Storm was curled up asleep next to her.

He seemed more like his normal self, but his sparkling midnight-blue eyes were still concerned. "I will stay here and hide. I want to be sure that Shadow cannot sense where I am," he barked.

Lily felt reluctant to leave him, but she

had promised to meet Adjoa at Greengates and help settle Pixie into her new home.

"I'll see you later," she said, bending down to kiss the top of Storm's warm silky head.

Storm curled himself into a tight ball and didn't answer.

"Whoa, there, girl!" Janie Green said gently.

Lily and Adjoa stood watching as Janie backed Pixie out of the horse trailer, hitched to her Land Rover. "That's it. Good. Come on."

Pixie slowly moved backward, step by step. Finally she stood in the stable yard, her legs trembling slightly and her chestnut coat twitching.

"Good girl," Adjoa said gently, going

over to pet Pixie's nose. "She's feeling nervous. She's been used to living in a field by herself."

"It's only natural for her to feel unsettled," Janie said understandingly.

"She's used to you, so why don't you and
Lily lead her around for a little before you
take her into the loose box? Call me if
you have any problems. Okay?"

"Okay. Thanks." Adjoa looked over at
Lily as Janie went to park her Land Rover.
"Janie's really nice, isn't she?"

Lily smiled and nodded. "There are
lots of strange new smells here. Why don't
you walk Pixie past the grazing field a few
times? It might calm her if she smells fresh
grass like in her field," she suggested to
Adjoa.

"That's a good idea."

For the next twenty minutes Adjoa led
Pixie around the yard, talking gently to
her the entire time.

Lily watched, trying not to think
about Storm and whether he was still safe.

But her worries about her tiny puppy
friend kept pushing into her mind.

Pixie gradually seemed to relax.
Finally, Adjoa felt confident enough to
lead her to Bandit's old loose box, which
was going to be her new home. Earlier,
Lily had covered it with a deep layer
of clean bedding. There was a hay net
hanging up and clean water in a bucket.

Lily opened the door wide.

Adjoa went to lead Pixie inside. But
Pixie rolled her eyes and stood still. "Come
on. It's lovely in there. There's space for
you to turn around and lie down if you
want to," she encouraged.

Pixie shifted nervously and rolled her
eyes. "She's just not comfortable with
going indoors," Adjoa said.

"I'll get some carrots from the feed

store. That might tempt her to go in," Lily said.

"Good idea," Adjoa said gratefully.

Lily returned quickly. But the carrots didn't work either.

"What if we can't get Pixie to go in at all?" Adjoa said worriedly. "Janie might change her mind about her. She won't want an awkward pony at the riding school."

"That's not going to happen. Pixie's just scared. She's going to be fine," Lily said reassuringly, but she was starting to get concerned.

If only Storm was here. He'd calm Pixie down. But Storm had to fight his own battle, hiding from his enemy—the fierce wolf Shadow.

"I think I'd better go and get Janie or

Don, after all," Lily decided reluctantly
after another fifteen minutes of leading
Pixie around and a second failed attempt
at getting her to go into her box.

"Okay, then." Adjoa was almost in
tears.

Just then Lily heard a rustling sound
from inside the loose box. A spurt of
bright golden sparks shot up out of the
straw and a cute sandy face appeared.

"Storm!" Lily exclaimed delightedly
and then realized that Adjoa was giving
her a strange look. "I mean . . . it looks like
rain or something. I think we should try
Pixie one more time before we go and get
help."

Adjoa looked doubtful, but she
nodded.

Pixie stretched out her neck and blew

a warm breath toward Storm. Storm barked encouragingly and wagged his tail.

Pixie lifted one front leg. She took a step forward and then another one. She went inside and Adjoa closed the door after her. "Phew! At last! I thought she'd never go in," she said, relieved.

"She'll be fine now. Why don't you go and tell Janie?" Lily suggested.

Just as Adjoa disappeared into the office, Storm whined in terror. He leaped over the stable door into the yard, trailing a bright comet's tail of golden sparks, and streaked toward the tack room.

Lily whipped around and saw two
small dogs coming through the main gates.
They raised their heads, and she saw their
abnormally long teeth and fierce pale wolf
eyes. Her heart skipped a beat. They were
here for Storm!

She dashed across the yard and rushed
into the empty tack room.

There was a bright golden flash. Lily
blinked hard as her vision cleared. Storm
stood there as his magnificent real self. The
majestic young wolf's dazzling silver-gray
fur gleamed, and his midnight-blue eyes
glowed like sapphires. A she-wolf with a
gentle tired face stood next to Storm.

And then Lily knew that this time
Storm was leaving for good.

"Our enemies are very close. We must

go!" Storm's mother rumbled.

Storm raised a large silver paw in farewell. "You have been a good friend. Be of good heart, Lily," he said in a deep velvety growl.

Lily's throat closed with tears and there was an ache in her chest. She was going to miss Storm terribly. "Good-bye, Storm. Take care. I'll never forget you," she whispered hoarsely.

There was a final bright flash and a crackle of gold sparks that sprinkled down around her like warm rain. Storm and his mother faded and then disappeared. The dogs ran into the tack room. Lily saw their teeth and eyes instantly return to normal before they turned and slunk away.

Lily blinked away tears as she went slowly back out into the yard. At least she'd had a chance to say good-bye to Storm. She knew she'd never forget the wonderful adventure she'd shared with the magic puppy.

Although she could never tell another person about Storm, there was someone else who was going to miss the tiny puppy and with whom she could share all her thoughts. Pixie!

As Lily went toward Pixie's stall and saw Adjoa coming out of Janie's office, she smiled at the thought of all the adventures they were going to have with their very own pony!

Magic Puppy

Muddy Paws

SUE BENTLEY

To Petra—gentle sheepdog friend
and a loyal companion.

Magic Puppy

Muddy Paws

SUE BENTLEY

Illustrated by Angela Swan

Grosset & Dunlap
An Imprint of Penguin Group (USA) LLC

Prologue

Storm paused to drink the clear water that flowed swiftly between two banks of ice. It felt good to be back in his home world.

But the young silver-gray wolf's happiness lasted for only a moment as he thought of his mother, Canista, wounded and in hiding.

Suddenly a terrifying howl echoed in the icy wind.

"Shadow!" Storm gasped, realizing that the fierce lone wolf was close.

Storm used his magic to transform himself quickly so he would be hidden from Shadow. There was a bright flash and a dazzling shower of golden sparks. Where Storm had been standing there now crouched a tiny fluffy black-and-white Border collie puppy with midnight-blue eyes.

Storm trembled, hoping that his puppy disguise would protect him from the evil Shadow. Keeping his little belly low to the ground, Storm crept into a clump of snow-covered bushes.

A dark shape pushed through the bushes, loosening a cloud of snow, and Storm's tiny heart missed a beat. Shadow had found him!

But instead of the lone wolf's dark-gray muzzle and pitiless black eyes, Storm saw a familiar silver-gray face with bright golden eyes.

"Mother!" he yapped with relief.

"I am glad you are safe and well, my son, but you have returned at a dangerous time," Canista said in a warm velvety growl. She nuzzled the disguised cub's black-and-white face, but then gave a sharp wince of pain.

"Shadow's poisonous bite sapped your strength!" Storm blew out a gentle stream of tiny gold sparks, which sank into Canista's injured leg and disappeared.

"Thank you, Storm. The pain is easing. But there's no time right now for you to help me recover all my powers. You must go—Shadow is very close," Canista rumbled softly.

Sadness rippled through Storm's tiny puppy body as he thought of his dead father and litter brothers and the once proud Moon-claw wolf pack, now broken up. His midnight-blue eyes flashed with anger. "One day I will stand beside you and face Shadow!"

Canista nodded proudly. "But until then, you must hide in the other world. Use this puppy disguise and return when your magic is stronger."

Another fierce howl split the air. "I know you are close, Storm! Come out and let us finish this!" Shadow cried in an icy growl.

"Go now, Storm! Save yourself!" Canista urged.

Bright gold sparks ignited in the

tiny black-and-white puppy's fur. Storm
whined softly as he felt the power
building inside him. Bright golden light
surrounded him. And grew brighter . . .

Chapter
ONE

Beth Hollis woke up with a start and lay looking up at the unfamiliar white ceiling with its low black beams. Rain pattered against the window, and she could hear animal noises and voices outside.

Gradually Beth recognized the attic bedroom in the Tail End Farm owned by her aunt and uncle. She was staying here while her parents were away.

The room was still dark, and a gust of wind sent more rain drumming against the window. Beth pulled the blanket over her head and snuggled back under the downy warmth.

Suddenly the bedroom door swung open. Beth heard muffled footsteps

approaching the bed and then she felt a
rush of cool air as the blanket was pulled
aside.

"Rise and shine!" cried a voice.
"Mornings start early on a farm!"

"Hey!" Beth complained, sitting
straight up.

Martin Badby, her tall dark-haired
cousin, stood grinning mischievously
down at her.

"Give that back!" Beth demanded,
lunging at him with outstretched arms.

"No way!" Martin yelled, backing
away. He tossed the blanket across the
room out of her reach.

Beth scowled. Martin was twelve
years old, older than her by three years,
but he sometimes acted as if he were six.
He loved playing silly jokes on people,

especially his younger cousin.

"That was a really mean thing to do!" she yelled.

"Yeah? So sue me!" Martin said cheerfully. "Are you coming downstairs, or what?"

Beth sat in the middle of her bed and crossed her arms. "No, I am not! Auntie Em said I didn't have to get up early on my first day here!"

"That's only 'cause you were sulking last night. I heard you talking to your mom and dad before they left. 'Poor me. It's *so* awful that I have to stay at boring Tail End,'" he mimicked in a silly whiny little voice.

"I don't talk like that!" Beth said, feeling her cheeks turn red. "Anyway, how would you like it if you got dumped on relatives while your parents flew to England for two weeks?"

Martin rolled his eyes. "They're not going anywhere fun, are they? It's just a boring business trip."

"I still wanted to go with them," Beth murmured. She'd never been away from her parents, except for the occasional sleepover at a friend's house, and she was really going to miss them.

"Talk about selfish. I guess you didn't even think about me?" Martin grumbled.

Beth frowned, puzzled. "What about you?"

"Well, *I* have to put up with *you*, don't I? Mom and Dad have practically ordered me to look after you. Just what I wanted, my stupid spoiled cousin following me around—not!"

"Thanks a lot! I'll try not to get in your way!" Beth cried indignantly. She flung herself off the bed and stomped over to the closet. "Can you leave now, please? I want to get dressed."

"I thought you weren't getting up?" Martin teased.

"I changed my mind. Spoiled cousins do that a lot, you know!" Beth said spiritedly.

"Whatever!" Martin went out and closed the bedroom door behind him.

Beth made a face at the closed door. She'd forgotten how annoying her cousin could be, and now it seemed that he wasn't happy having her here at all. Her spirits sank even further as she thought of the two weeks stretching endlessly ahead of her.

"Morning, Beth. You're up early. Did you sleep well?" Emily Badby called from the yard as Beth stood in the open doorway of the back porch.

"Fine, thanks," Beth replied. *No thanks to Martin*, she thought.

Her aunt held a bucket of vegetables.
"Goats love fresh food. It gets them in a
good mood for milking. Do you want to
come and watch?"

"Okay," Beth said, shrugging. She
wasn't that interested in goats, but there
was still so much time before breakfast
and nothing else to do.

She borrowed a pair of boots and
followed her aunt into the barn. A sweet
musty smell of goats, dung, and warm
hay greeted her. "Phew!" Beth said as she
wrinkled her nose.

Emily Badby laughed. "It's a healthy
farm smell. You'll get used to it."

Beth wasn't sure she wanted to. She
went to look at the brown-and-white
goats in their pens, down one side of the
barn. "They all look a little annoyed. What

kind are they?" she asked.

"Anglo-Nubians. It's their long noses
and floppy ears that give them that
expression," Emily explained, selecting
a goat and leading it to a small wooden
platform. The goat leaped up nimbly, and
soon Beth was watching the creamy milk
foaming into a clean bucket. "I sell milk,
yogurt, and cheese in the local stores,"
Emily said. "My dairy's next door. You can
have a look around sometime, but ask me
first. I have strict rules about hygiene."

Beth nodded.

When her aunt finished milking, she
poured the milk through a filter into a
metal churn. "I'll just take this to the dairy
and then get started on breakfast."

A loud braying noise came from the
back of the barn. "Oh! What's that?" Beth

looked around in surprise.

Her aunt laughed. "That's Darcy, my
new billy goat. He's only been here for a
week or so, but he's always complaining
because he isn't getting any attention."

"Can I go and say hello to him?" Beth
asked.

"Yes, of course, but be——" The rest
of her aunt's reply was drowned out by a
loud irritable voice in the doorway.

"There you are!" Martin cried,
standing aside as his mom left. "What are
you hiding in here for?"

"I wasn't hiding! Auntie Em said I
could watch her milking," Beth said.

Martin flicked back a strand of wet
dark hair. "Anyway, Dad said I had to ask
you if you wanted to come with me to
take Ella for a walk." Ella was the family's

old black-and-white Welsh Border collie.

"No thanks," Beth said, feeling annoyed that he'd only asked her because his dad had made him. Turning on her heel, she went toward the back of the barn. "I'm going to look at Darcy."

"Hang on! I'll come with you. Ella won't mind waiting for her walk. I have to drag her out half the time anyway. Since Dad retired her from farm work, she's really stiffened up," Martin said.

Darcy's pen was behind some straw bales. He was a handsome dark-brown goat with a white neck. "It looks like he's wearing a cute white collar!" Beth exclaimed as Darcy lifted his head and gave an inquisitive snicker.

Martin undid the latch and gestured for Beth to go into the pen ahead of him.

Beth hesitated. "Are you sure it's safe to go in?"

"'Course," Martin said. "Are you chicken or what?"

Beth took two steps into the pen. Suddenly, she felt Martin shove her in the back and heard the gate slam shut.

She shot forward and almost went sprawling in the straw.

"You idiot!" she cried, turning around just in time to see Martin jogging away through the barn. "That's not funny!" she shouted after him.

There was a noise from behind her. Beth turned to see Darcy curling his lips and eyeing her suspiciously.

She swallowed. "N-nice goat."

Darcy lowered his head. He looked like he was going to charge!

Chapter
TWO

Beth's heart rose into her mouth.
Suddenly there was a dazzling flash of
gold light, and a big shower of bright
gold sparks sprinkled all around her and
Darcy. Blinded for a moment, she rubbed
her eyes. Beth tensed as she felt a peculiar
warm, tingly feeling down her spine.

When she could see again, she noticed
that Darcy was frozen where he stood,

and standing between the goat's legs was
a tiny fluffy black-and-white puppy with
enormous midnight-blue eyes. Specks
of gold dust seemed to be glimmering
around its fur.

"What's going on?" Beth exclaimed.

The tiny puppy drew itself up. "I am
Storm, of the Moon-claw pack. I have
arrived from a place that is far from here."

"Y–you can talk?" Beth gasped in total
amazement.

Suddenly, Beth had a realization. This was obviously another one of her cousin's practical jokes. She looked around, expecting Martin to jump out triumphantly.

But there was no sign of him. Beth slowly looked back to where Storm was blinking up at her, and Darcy was still standing as if he were carved from stone.

"I don't get this," she said, puzzled.

The fluffy black-and-white puppy took a few steps toward her on big soft paws that seemed too large for his tiny body. "I used my magic to stop this animal before it could hurt you," Storm woofed. "Who are you?"

"I'm B–Beth H–Hollis," Beth stammered.

Storm bowed his head. "I am honored to meet you, Beth."

Beth was still having trouble taking all of this in. "Um . . . me too. But . . . who are you? *What* are you?"

Storm didn't answer. Instead, there was another bright golden flash.

"Oh!" Beth found herself outside Darcy's pen. Behind her the goat snickered contentedly, and she heard him moving around in the straw as if nothing had happened.

Beth looked around for the puppy. But it had disappeared, and standing in its place outside the pen with her there crouched a magnificent young silver-gray wolf with glowing midnight-blue eyes. Large gold sparks glowed in the thick ruff around his neck.

Beth gasped, eyeing the wolf's sharp teeth. "Storm?"

"Yes, it is me, Beth. Do not be afraid,"
Storm said in a deep velvety growl.

Before Beth could get used to the
sight of the amazing young wolf there
was a final dazzling flash of gold light and
Storm was once again a tiny fluffy black-
and-white puppy.

"Wow! That's an amazing disguise.

No one would ever know you're a wolf!"
Beth exclaimed. "But who are you hiding
from?"

Storm began to tremble all over, and
his deep-blue eyes glowed with anger and
fear. "Shadow is a fierce lone wolf who
killed my father and all my brothers and
wounded my mother with his poisonous
bite. Now Shadow is looking for me. Can
you help me, Beth?"

"Of course I will!" Beth's soft heart
went out to him. Storm was impressive
as a young wolf, but he was adorable as
a tiny helpless puppy. She bent down to
pick him up. "I'll ask Auntie Em if you
can stay in my room," she said, petting his
soft little ears.

Storm leaned up to lick her chin.
"Thank you, Beth."

"Just wait until I tell Martin about you! He's going to be so jealous!"

"No, Beth! You can't tell anyone my secret!" Storm said, his tiny black-and-white face very serious.

Beth didn't want to do anything that would put her new friend in danger. Besides, she reasoned, Martin had been such a pain recently that he didn't deserve to know about Storm anyway. "Okay, then," she decided. "It's just you and me. I promise."

"Aren't you a little too old to be talking to an imaginary friend?" Martin said, suddenly appearing from behind the straw bales. His eyes widened when he saw Storm. "Where did that cute puppy come from?"

"I just found him. He said his name's—"

Beth stopped quickly as she realized that
she was going to have to be a lot more
careful about keeping Storm's secret. "I
mean I'm going to call him Storm."

Martin's face softened for an instant.
"Ella looked just like that when she was
a puppy. He must be a Border collie, too.
Let me hold him."

"I think I'll hold on to him. He's still a
little scared," Beth said.

Martin frowned. "No one would

think he's yours. This is my barn, so Storm obviously belongs to me. Hand him over!" he ordered.

Beth hesitated, annoyed at being bossed around again. Martin didn't even bother to ask if she was okay after he'd shoved her into Darcy's pen.

"Do not worry, Beth. Do as he says," Storm woofed.

Beth blinked in astonishment. What was Storm doing, talking to her when Martin was so close? But her cousin didn't seem to have noticed anything strange. *I hope you know what you're doing, Storm*, she thought as she reluctantly held him out toward Martin.

Smiling triumphantly, Martin went to grab Storm, but the moment he touched his black-and-white fur he jumped backward.

"Ye-oww!" he yelled, shaking his hands
in the air. "Something just stung me!
Does he have a stinging bug in his fur or
something?"

Beth pulled Storm back and held him
closely again. "I'll take a look. Maybe you
should go and ask Auntie Em for some
antiseptic cream."

"Er . . . yeah." Martin nodded as he
went off, still rubbing at his hands.

"Storm!" Beth scolded gently. "You

gave him a prick from your invisible gold
sparks, didn't you?"

Storm's blue eyes twinkled
mischievously. "I think I may have made
them a bit too sharp. But the feeling will
soon wear off," he woofed.

"Serves Martin right. Maybe he'll
think twice before grabbing you again!
But how come he didn't hear you speak to
me just now?" Beth asked, puzzled.

"I used my magic, so that only you
can hear me." Storm snuggled up in Beth's
arms.

"You can do that? So I can hear you,
but everyone else just hears you barking?
Cool!" Beth kissed the top of his soft
little head. "Let's go and find Auntie Em.
Breakfast should be almost ready. I bet
you're hungry after your long journey."

Storm's tummy rumbled and he gave an eager little bark.

As Beth went toward the farmhouse, she smiled. Her boring two weeks at Tail End Farm looked like they were going to be a lot more fun with Storm around!

Chapter
THREE

"I wonder where he came from,"
Emily said thoughtfully after Beth finished
telling her about Storm. "We're pretty far
from any houses out here."

Beth looked across to where Storm
was chomping on a dish of dog food. Ella,
the old collie, lay curled in her basket
watching the puppy.

"I bet Storm was abandoned. His

owners were probably hoping some kind
person would give him a home. Like you,
Auntie Em," Beth said hopefully.

"I really hate people who treat animals
like that," Martin said.

"Me too!" Beth said with feeling. It
was the first time she and Martin had
agreed on anything.

They all sat at the kitchen table, eating
their huge farmhouse breakfasts and
drinking big mugs of tea.

"I'm not sure it's a good time to have
a stray puppy getting under everyone's
feet," Beth's uncle said. "We're very busy
on the farm and no one has time to train
him. Maybe we should take Storm straight
to the pet care center."

Beth's heart pounded. He couldn't
mean it! She just found Storm—she

couldn't bear to lose her new friend so quickly.

Suddenly Ella gave a rusty-sounding bark. She got up and limped stiffly over to Storm. The tiny puppy whined softly, wagging his tail and wriggling his fat little body as the old dog bent down and gave him an experimental sniff. Ella's eyes softened and she began licking Storm's head.

Martin's face lit up. "Look at that! Ella's telling us that she'll keep Storm in check. She won't let him be a pest around the farm. Way to go, old girl!"

Everyone laughed.

Beth looked at her uncle and aunt. "So, can Storm stay? He can live in my room and I'll take him home when Mom and Dad come to get me," she pleaded.

"In that case, it's fine with me. If it's okay with you, Emily," Oliver said to his wife.

Beth's aunt gave a questionable smile, but she nodded.

Beth went over and hugged her aunt and uncle. "Yay! Thanks a million!"

She felt so happy that she was even ready to forgive Martin for playing mean tricks on her, but there was still one thing she wanted to mention to him first.

Beth waited until she, Martin, Storm, and Ella were walking across the fields before bringing the subject up. "I think you should apologize for pushing me into Darcy's pen. It was a mean thing to do," she exclaimed.

Martin's eyes widened. "Are you still talking about that? Can't you take a joke? Girls *always* make such a big deal out of everything."

"Yes, because boys do such stupid things!" Beth replied. "I thought Darcy was going to charge at me. If it hadn't been for St—Anyway, I was lucky to get out without getting hurt."

But Martin wasn't listening. He had turned around to wait for Ella, who was lagging behind. The old collie was walking stiffly with her head drooping. "Come on, girl!" he called fondly.

At the sound of his voice, Ella tried to quicken her step, but her back legs gave way and she sat down.

"She's been doing that more and more lately," Martin said, frowning.

Beth's anger with Martin melted away as her heart filled with sadness at the sight of the sick old dog.

Storm glanced up at her with softly glowing eyes. "I will fetch Ella!" he woofed gently.

Beth stood beside Martin and they watched Storm bound down the field. As soon as Storm reached the old sheepdog, he barked encouragingly and licked Ella's gray muzzle. When she just lay there panting, Storm crouched down onto his front paws and stuck his bottom in the air, inviting her to play chase.

Martin smiled at the cute puppy's antics. "You're wasting your time, Storm. Ella's running around days are *well* over!" he called, but then his face fell and his eyes looked sad and troubled.

Beth reached out to touch his arm.

"I'm okay. Don't make a scene!" Martin said, rubbing a sleeve across his face.

Beth saw Storm running back and forth in front of Ella, woofing gently to encourage her until she finally heaved herself to her feet. As the old collie limped up the field, Storm ambled alongside her, keeping pace on his short legs.

"Here she comes. Good girl," Martin said, petting Ella's ears.

"Thanks, Storm," Beth whispered to him. "Martin might be the most annoying person in the universe, but he really loves Ella."

The four of them slowly walked back to the farmyard in silence. As they came through the gate into the yard, Martin turned to Beth. "Do you want to see the dairy?" he said more cheerfully.

Beth shrugged. "I don't care. But I thought we weren't allowed in there without permission."

"No problem. I told Mom we might go in and she was cool with it." Martin opened the door of a brick building, next to the barn. "But dogs are definitely not allowed. Stay, Ella," he ordered.

Ella sat down obediently.

"Will you wait here, please, Storm?"

Beth whispered, so Martin couldn't hear. "I won't be long."

Storm immediately sat down next to Ella and lay with his nose on his paws.

Martin smiled. "Storm really catches on quickly, doesn't he? Look how he copies what Ella does. He's one bright puppy!"

Beth smiled to herself. If only Martin knew how right he was!

Inside the dairy it was cool and really clean. Beth walked around, looking at the white work surfaces, shiny metal equipment, and huge fridges, being careful not to touch anything.

But Martin was just the opposite. "I haven't been in here for so long. I forgot that some of this stuff's pretty high-tech. I wonder what these do." He began turning some dials on a big drum-shaped machine.

There was an ominous glugging noise.

"Should you be playing with that?"
Beth asked worriedly.

Martin grinned. "You're such a
scaredy-cat. Don't panic. I'm putting the
settings back to what they were." He
turned the dial again and the glugging
noise got louder.

Gloop. Gloop. Whoosh!

Suddenly a fountain of milk gushed
out of a narrow chute and poured onto
the floor.

"Oh no!" Martin cried, frantically
working, but the milk only sprayed out
faster.

Beth stood there in horror as a rising
tide of milk swirled around her boots. "Do
something, Martin!"

"I'm trying to!" Martin's face was
bright red.

The door banged open and Emily
Badby rushed into the dairy. Taking in
the situation with one look, she marched
over to the machine and adjusted the dials.
Seconds later, the flow of milk slowed and
then stopped.

Emily turned around with a furious look on her face.

"Beth told me to do it!" Martin cried, before his mom could speak.

Beth's jaw dropped. "No, I didn't!"

Martin smirked. "Yes, you did! Don't try and squirm your way out of it—"

"Be quiet! Both of you," Emily snapped. "I'm very disappointed in you both. You're not even supposed to be in here without permission!"

Beth glared furiously at Martin. She was really tempted to tell her aunt how he had lied about having permission to come in here, but she'd never been a tattletale and she wasn't about to start now.

"You know the house rules perfectly well, Martin. Besides, Beth is our guest," Emily said stiffly, still furious. "What do you have to say for yourself?"

Martin shrugged. "Chill out, Mom! Don't have a major panic attack! It's only a little milk. It won't take long to clean up."

"You think so?" Emily's face darkened. "Stay there, you two! Don't you dare move!" She sloshed through the milk and opened a cabinet. "Here!" She thrust mops and buckets at Martin and Beth. "I want that floor spotless. Do you hear me? I'd stand and watch you, but I have to go out now. I'll be back in an hour, though, to check up on you. And if you touch anything else, Martin Badby, you'll . . . you'll be in big trouble!"

She stormed out, and a few seconds later Beth heard a car start up and drive away.

"Oh gosh!" Beth said, letting out a huge sigh of relief. She'd never seen her aunt so angry. "I thought she was going to explode!"

"Oh, Mom's never angry for long. She'll forget all about it by this evening. You don't mind cleaning up by yourself, do you? I just remembered I've got something important to talk to Dad about," Martin said, splashing milk everywhere as he went toward the door.

"Hey! Come back—" Beth cried, but Martin had already left.

Her spirits sank as she looked down at the lake of milk. It was everywhere: under the work surfaces, sloshing around the machinery, and even leaking out under the door into the yard. She hardly knew where to begin.

"Thanks for nothing, Martin," she grumbled, angry that she'd bothered to save him from being in even more trouble with her aunt.

"I will help you, Beth!" Storm woofed eagerly from the open doorway.

Beth felt a warm prickling sensation down her spine. Something very strange was about to happen.

Big gold sparks ignited in Storm's
fluffy black-and-white fur, and his ears
and tail crackled with electricity.

Storm raised a big black front paw,
and a spurt of golden sparks shot out and
whooshed around the dairy. They zizzed
around like a swarm of busy worker bees.

Beth heard a series of faint pops as a
shimmering army of mops appeared out

of thin air and stood at attention. As if at
an invisible signal, they began mopping the
floor up and down in neat rows. In perfect
time, they squeezed their milky heads into
each bucket in turn. *Swish! Swoosh!*

"This is great!" Beth said, clapping her
hands with glee as the rows of mops did
their work.

In no time at all, the dairy floor was
spotless. The magic mops stood at

attention once more and then disappeared in a final cascade of golden sparks.

"Wow! Thanks, Storm, that was awesome!" Beth went over and gave him a cuddle.

"You are welcome," Storm barked happily. "But I saw Martin going into the house. Why didn't he help you?"

"That's what I want to know," Beth said angrily. "He made some lame excuse about talking to his dad about something. I've had just about enough of my annoying cousin. Come on, Storm, let's go and find him. I've got a few things I want to say to him!"

Storm yapped in agreement.

As Beth charged into the house with Storm toward the living room, she heard Uncle Ollie's voice coming through the open door and stopped in her tracks.

"It's really not fair to let Ella go on like this. She's in pain and she can barely move around. I think it's time we called the vet and put her to sleep," he was saying.

"No! Please wait, Dad. Let's leave her for just a little longer," Martin pleaded, sounding as if he was very close to tears.

"I'm sorry, Martin. I know you love Ella, but I'm not prepared to let any animal suffer, however hard it is for you to accept. We have to think what's best for Ella. Why don't we talk about it again tomorrow. All right?" Oliver Badby said gently.

"Okay. But I'm not changing my mind about calling the vet and you can't make me!" Martin said in a choked voice.

Beth didn't wait to hear the rest of the conversation. She already felt a little guilty for listening. "Come on, Storm," she whispered, tiptoeing away.

Storm trotted at her heel as she went into the kitchen. Beth felt her anger drain away again, just like when they were in the field earlier. However annoying her cousin was, she wouldn't wish that on anyone.

"Martin was actually telling the truth this time. He really did want to talk to his dad about something important. Ella must be very sick if Uncle Ollie thinks the vet should put her to sleep. Poor old girl," she said to Storm.

Storm nodded, his midnight-blue eyes sad.

Ella was curled up in her basket in the warm alcove. As Beth bent down to pet her, the old dog's tail thumped against the floor.

Beth felt tears stinging her eyes. "It's a shame that Ella's in such pain. If she wasn't, she'd be able to enjoy a few more months with Martin."

Storm pricked his ears. "I might be able to help!"

Beth blinked at him. "Really? Can you use your magic to make her young again?" she asked hopefully.

"I am sorry, Beth. No magic can do that," Storm woofed gently. He padded over and stood in front of Ella.

Once again, Beth felt the warm tingling sensation down her spine.

Big gold sparks ignited in Storm's fluffy black-and-white fur and the tips of his ears sparked with magical power. She watched as he huffed out a warm glittery breath.

A shimmering golden mist surrounded the old collie. For a few seconds, pinpricks of gold danced all around her like miniature fireflies and

then they sank into Ella's dull fur and
disappeared.

Beth waited expectantly, but nothing
happened. Ella looked just the same, with
her gray muzzle and faded eyes.

Storm's magic didn't seem to have
worked.

"Never mind. You tried. I guess magic
can't be expected to do everything,"
Beth said to Storm, trying hard to hide
her disappointment as the last golden
spark faded from Ella's fur. "Let's go into
the living room and find Martin. He's

probably feeling really upset. Maybe we can cheer him up."

Storm had a gleam in his eye, but he just nodded. "You have a very kind heart, Beth."

"Anyone would do the same," Beth said, blushing. She always got embarrassed when people gave her compliments.

Martin was lying on the sofa. Behind it, Beth could see the cabinet displaying the cups and trophies her uncle had won in plowing competitions.

Oliver Badby sat at the table, working at the computer. He looked up and smiled as Beth and Storm came in. "Hello. What have you two been up to?"

"We . . . I've finished cleaning up all the milk in the dairy. I thought Martin might like to go out with us or something," Beth said.

Her uncle frowned and glanced at Martin. "What's that about milk?"

"Er . . . nothing!" Martin said hurriedly, getting up in a rush and pushing Beth out. "Come on, Beth. Let's go and see if Mom needs any help with her shopping."

"But she's not even back yet . . ." Beth protested, shaking off his arm.

"Duh! I know that! But Dad doesn't, does he?" Martin scoffed. "And why did you have to mention the milk?"

But once in the hall, his shoulders slumped. "Dad's been talking about taking Ella to the vet, to . . . to—"

"I know. I heard you talking to him," Beth interrupted, feeling a lump rise in her throat. "I'm so sorry."

Martin shuffled his feet. "Yeah, well.
I know Ella's old and everything and I'm
not ready to let her go, but Dad could
be ..." He lifted his head and looked
past Beth into the kitchen. She saw an
expression of complete amazement come
over his face. "I don't believe it!"

"What?" Beth whipped around and

saw Ella padding out of the kitchen.
The old dog was moving easily. Her coat
looked glossy and her eyes were bright
and alert.

Ella trotted up to Martin and jumped
up to be petted. "Woof!" she barked
happily, wagging her tail and giving him a
wide doggy grin.

"Look at her! It's like a miracle. She's
not even limping!" Martin threw his arms
around Ella and hugged her, burying his
face in her fur.

Ella barked, licking him all over his
face.

"Just wait until Dad sees her! There's
no way he'll be taking her to the vet
now!" Martin's face was lit up like a
Halloween pumpkin.

Beth beamed with joy as she watched

the two of them. She bent down to pet
Storm. "Thanks again, Storm. This time
from Martin and Ella. They're going
to have a great summer together," she
whispered.

Storm wagged his little tail happily.

C h a p t e r
FIVE

"Ella seems to have found a new
best friend since that puppy arrived,"
Emily Badby said as she was clearing away
lunch the following day.

Beth was helping her aunt load the
dishwasher. She smiled, wishing that
everyone knew just how true that was!
But, of course, she would never tell them
or anyone else how magical Storm was.

Oliver Badby was finishing a cup of tea, and Martin had just come back into the kitchen after taking some food scraps outside to the pigpen.

Storm was stretched out under the table. Suddenly his eyes flashed with mischief. Leaping out, he ran around the huge farmhouse table, his ears laid back and his tail streaming behind him.

Across the room in her bed, Ella's ears pricked up. With a spring in her step, she shot toward the silly puppy and started chasing him. Storm suddenly swerved, leaped into her empty bed, and threw himself down. Ella jumped straight in after him. Seconds later, the two of them were curled up together, licking each other.

Everyone laughed.

"That's one way to sneak into a warm

bed! You know, Ella and Storm could
almost be a mother and her puppy,"
Martin said fondly.

Then they heard the rumbling sound
of a heavy truck pulling up outside in
the yard. Martin ran to the window and
looked out.

"It's here, Dad! The Fergy's arrived!"
he shouted, dashing outside.

Beth's uncle and aunt went outside to

look. Beth followed curiously, wondering
what was going on.

A large flatbed truck stood in the yard.
On the back of it, there was a tomato-red
tractor. Oliver went to speak to the truck
driver, and then they began the unloading.
A few minutes later, the red tractor stood
in the yard.

Martin walked around it, his eyes
shining. "It's supercool, isn't it?"

"I guess it's okay," Beth said, shrugging.
She couldn't see what was so exciting
about a boring old farm machine.

"Okay?" Martin gave her an
incredulous look. "Are you kidding? That's
a 1952 Massey Ferguson tractor."

Beth wasn't impressed. "It's kind of
old, isn't it? Does it still work?"

Her uncle chuckled. "Fergy's going

to work very well. Wait until you see her pulling a plow. She's going to help me win the cup in the vintage class at the plowing competition in a few weeks."

"Dad's county champion at plowing," Martin said proudly.

To Beth, winning things for making straight lines down a field seemed like a very weird thing to do. *Don't they watch any TV around here?* she thought.

Martin saw the scornful look on her face. He blushed. "There's a lot of skill involved in plowing, you know. Dad lets me try sometimes and I'm getting really good at it," he boasted. "I'm going to get a license when I'm fourteen. Then I can compete, too!"

"You're doing all right, but you'll need a lot more practice first," his dad said.

"I know that," Martin said in a sulky voice.

Oliver patted his son on the shoulder. "Fergy could use a wash and brush up. She's pretty dusty after her journey. Any volunteers?"

Martin's head came up. "Beth and I will do it. Won't we, Beth?"

Beth frowned. Cleaning a tractor was definitely not on the top of her "fun to do" list. It was right at the bottom, next to cleaning smelly sneakers. But Martin seemed in an unusually good mood, so she nodded.

"Okay. I don't mind." *But if he starts bossing me around again, I'm leaving him to do it*, she thought.

Beth helped Martin collect buckets, sponges, and cleaning liquid. Storm came outside and lay down with his chin resting on his paws as she and Martin started work.

"There's all kinds of plowing, you know. Tractor-trailed, mounted, reversible. You have to be very skilled to work a plot and make perfect ins and outs," Martin explained enthusiastically as he sponged soapy water over Fergy's bright-red hood. "They have world championship competitions. One day Dad might be good enough to participate."

Beth didn't reply. She was scrubbing hard at a greasy mark on Fergy's red grill.

"Hey! Are you listening? Or are you ignoring me on purpose?" Martin flicked soapy water at her.

"Who said that?" Beth joked and flicked water back at him.

Martin's eyes gleamed mischievously. "Oh yeah!"

Beth dodged out of the way as another sponge full of water flew toward her. "Missed!" she teased.

Laughing, they flicked soapy water back and forth.

Beth giggled as she pushed her damp hair out of her eyes and crouched behind the tractor. She was smaller than Martin and managed to avoid getting too wet, but most of her soapy flicks found their mark.

Martin's T-shirt was soon drenched.
"Right! Now you're in for it!" He
grabbed the whole bucket and lifted it
into the air.

"Don't you dare!" Beth shrieked
breathlessly.

As she went to flick more water at

Martin, a tiny shower of golden sparks
crackled around her hand and tingled
against her fingers. The soapy sponge
shot out of her hand. It zoomed through
the air with perfect aim and splatted in
Martin's face.

"Phoof!" Martin spluttered. He took
a step backward and slipped over onto
his backside, tipping the entire bucket of
water all over himself.

Beth cracked up laughing. She was
helpless. She glanced across at Storm, who
wore a wide doggy grin, and wagged her
finger at him, scolding him gently.

"Sorry, Beth. I thought he was going
to hurt you!" Storm yapped.

Scowling, Martin slowly got up. His
dark hair was plastered to his head, and
water was dripping off the end of his nose.

Beth tried to stop laughing at the look on Martin's face, but her mouth kept twitching. "You should see yourself," she gasped, holding her ribs.

Suddenly Martin burst out laughing, too. "That was a great shot—for a girl! Come on, let's get some clean water."

Beth went with him to fill her bucket from the outside tap. Staying at Tail End Farm was starting to feel a lot better these days.

She was amazed at Martin. This was the most friendly he'd been since she arrived. And all because they'd had a water fight and she'd beaten him. *I'll never understand boys*, she thought as they finished cleaning the tractor.

Chapter
SIX

Beth stood in the barn beside her aunt
and watched her milking the goats. Storm
was sprawled on a pile of clean straw
beside the pens.

Beth sighed. It had rained almost every
day since she'd been here. Heavy rain was
drumming on the roof once again. "I'm
getting fed up with this terrible weather,"
she complained.

Emily smiled. "You learn to deal with it when you work on a farm. But the goats really hate the cold and the wet. That's why I brought them into the barn, but I'd hoped they could go out in their field again by now." She looked at her niece's sad face. "Do you want to try milking?"

"I don't know," Beth said doubtfully.

"Come on. Don't be shy. Stand here. It's not very difficult and Daisy's a good milker," Emily encouraged. She showed Beth how to take a firm but gentle hold and squeeze down with one finger at a time.

Beth took a deep breath and rested one shoulder against Daisy's flank. She followed instructions, a bit awkwardly at first. To her surprise, the milk began to flow into the bucket.

"Hey! I'm doing it!" she cried delightedly.

In a few minutes Beth felt like an expert. She filled a bucket and then strained the milk into the metal churn, feeling really pleased with her success. "That was great. Maybe I'll ask Mom and Dad if we can have some goats. It would save Dad moaning about having to dig up all the weeds, and we'd have tons of milk to give to all our friends."

"Hmm. Remember that you'd have
to milk them twice a day, summer and
winter, seven days a week, in all kinds of
weather, just like I do," her aunt cautioned,
smiling.

Beth raised her eyebrows. "On second
thought, I think I'll stick to milk in
cartons and leave the weeds to Dad!"

Her aunt laughed.

A loud triumphant braying came
from the back of the barn. There was a
stamping and clattering, followed by a
rustling noise.

"Darcy?! What's he doing?" Beth
asked.

"It sounds like he's jumped out of his
pen—again," her aunt sighed. "That goat's
a real menace. He's been cooped up for

too long because of all this rain and he's got energy to spare. It's going to be really hard to catch him."

"Can I help you?" Beth offered.

"You could go and see where Darcy's gone, if you like, while I close the barn door so he can't escape," her aunt said.

"I will find Darcy!" Storm barked, darting to the back of the barn.

Beth hurried after him. As she reached the big stack of straw bales near the goat's pen, she spotted Darcy standing right on the very top of them.

"Look at him! He thinks he's the king of the castle!" Beth said.

Looking down his haughty nose, Darcy snickered as if he agreed. He looked very pleased with himself for having climbed up so high.

Storm wagged his tail and then jumped up onto his back legs and put his front paws on the bottom bale.

"Gr-oof!" his bright eyes flashed playfully.

"Watch out, Storm. That stack looks a little wobbly—" Beth began, but before she could finish her sentence, Darcy flexed his powerful back legs and did an almighty leap in the air, right over Beth and Storm's heads—and then everything seemed to happen all at once.

The top straw bale shook wildly from the force of Darcy's takeoff and slowly began to tip forward.

Beth's eyes widened in horror. Storm had turned his head to watch Darcy land on the barn floor a few feet away and hadn't noticed the danger. The bale was about to fall and land on him!

Without a second thought, Beth threw herself forward. Her fingers just touched Storm's fluffy black-and-white fur and she managed to grab him. Holding him close to her chest Beth rolled out of the way just in time. The heavy bale crashed to the ground, and she felt the rush of dusty air as it missed them both by a fraction of an inch.

Beth let out a shaky sigh of relief. Still holding Storm, she pushed herself slowly to her feet. "Are you all right?" she asked the shocked little puppy.

"Yes. You saved me, Beth. Thank you," Storm woofed, reaching up to lick her chin.

"I couldn't bear anything happening to you," Beth said as she petted Storm's soft ears. She felt a surge of affection for her tiny friend.

Glancing down the barn, Beth saw that her aunt had managed to get a rope on a subdued-looking Darcy and was leading him back to his pen. She frowned when she reached Beth and Storm and saw the straw bale on the floor nearby. "I thought I heard something fall, but I couldn't be sure with all the noise Darcy was making. Are you okay? You're lucky you weren't badly hurt," she said.

"Oh, it missed us by miles," Beth said lightly, not wanting to worry her aunt.

"Thank goodness for that!" Emily said, relieved. "I'm responsible for you while you're here, and your mom and dad

wouldn't be very happy with me if you
had an accident. I'll get Oliver to come
and fix that stack. Just let me tether this
naughty goat in his pen first. He's full of
surprises."

Beth bit back a grin. *He's not the only
one!* she thought.

"I'm sorry, Martin, I don't have time
to go out with you today. Maybe
tomorrow. I'm planning to clear the
unused part of the top field and use
that for practicing plowing, but I can't
promise when I'll get around to it,"
Oliver was saying.

"Aw, Da-ad. You've already been out
on Fergy a couple of times. When am I
going to get the chance to take a drive?"

Beth sat in the window seat in the

living room with Storm curled on a
cushion beside her. Her uncle and cousin
were in the yard outside. Their voices
floated in through the open window.
"Martin's obsessed with that dumb old
red tractor, even though Uncle Ollie
told him it's too big for him to drive by
himself."

Storm's ears twitched and he gave
a sleepy nod, tired out from all the
excitement in the barn earlier.

Two minutes later, Martin burst into
the room and threw himself down next
to Beth.

"Watch it! You almost sat on Storm!"
Beth complained.

"Sorry, Storm." Martin petted Storm's
fluffy black-and-white fur absently. "Dad's
being a big pain! He won't let me near

Fergy unless he's with me. I know I can handle driving her by myself, but he won't believe me," he grumbled.

Beth wisely chose to stay silent on the subject. "It finally stopped raining. Why don't we walk into the village with Storm and Ella?" she suggested, trying to cheer him up.

Martin's lip curled. "Go shopping? I'd rather watch paint dry. I'm going to take Ella for a long walk over the fields. By myself," he said rudely.

Beth got the message. She didn't bother to tell him that she was about to suggest that they go to the new sports center. "Suit yourself." She shrugged, got up, and called to Storm to follow her.

"Where are you going?" Martin asked, frowning.

Beth turned to him and tapped the side of her nose with one finger in what she knew was an annoying way.

Martin threw up his hands, got up, and stormed out, muttering about "stupid annoying girls" under his breath.

"Oh well. Martin's back to his usual self. His good mood didn't last long, did it?" Beth said to Storm. "But I'm getting used to him now and I don't mind it so much. I think he just likes complaining!"

Storm nodded, blinking up at her with bright midnight-blue eyes.

Beth changed her mind about the sports center. "We'll go to the village by ourselves. I bet they have a pet shop that sells dog treats," she decided.

Storm yelped excitedly, almost falling over his own paws as he bounded out of the door.

Chapter
SEVEN

Emily Badby had been baking bread
all morning, and the whole farmhouse
smelled wonderful.

Beth sat in the cozy kitchen, reading
a new computer magazine she'd bought
at the village shop. Storm was curled
up under the table, chewing on a bone-
shaped dog chew, and Beth could feel the
tiny puppy's warmth against her feet.

It had just been raining again, but a watery sun was now beginning to push through the clouds.

Suddenly the faint sound of barking and growling interrupted Beth's peaceful morning. She tensed up, listening hard. It seemed to be coming from far away, but then the noise stopped and Beth thought she must have been mistaken. Her aunt didn't seem to have noticed anything.

"Where's Martin?" Beth asked.

"Up at the top field. His dad's starting to clear it with Fergy and the old plow. Ella's with him," Emily replied.

Making sure her aunt wasn't looking, Beth leaned over to whisper to Storm. "I'll take you for a walk up there later. It's no good waiting for Martin and Ella to come back here. Wild horses wouldn't drag him away if Uncle Ollie's plowing."

There was no reply.

Frowning, Beth bent over and looked under the table. Storm was gone, leaving the half-eaten dog chew lying there.

That was odd. He'd never run off without telling her where he was going before. She got up and went to look for him.

Storm wasn't in the living room or any of the other downstairs rooms. She went up to her bedroom, expecting to find him curled up on her blanket, but he wasn't there either.

"Storm?" she said, beginning to feel concerned.

A faint sound came from under her pillows. Beth smiled and pulled back the top of the blanket to reveal a little black-and-white tail. "What's this, hide-and-seek—" she began, but stopped at the sight of Storm trembling all over. "What's wrong? Are you sick?" she asked worriedly.

Storm squirmed farther into the pillows. "I sense that Shadow knows where I am. He will send his magic, so that any dogs that are nearby will attack me," he said in a muffled little whine.

"Oh no! That must have been what I heard. We need to find you a better hiding place. Maybe the barn or . . . or . . ." Beth tried to think of somewhere safe.

"It is no use, Beth," Storm whimpered, his deep-blue eyes as dull as stones. "Leave me here for a while, please. Any dogs looking for me may pass by."

"All right. If that's what you want," Beth said. She had a sudden thought. "What about Ella? Will Shadow's magic work on her, too?" She felt horrified that the gentle old collie might become Storm's enemy.

"No. I have already used my magic to help her. That will protect Ella from Shadow's evil ways," Storm whined before he burrowed right under the pillows and curled up into a tight little ball.

Beth gently gathered his tail in, replaced the blanket, and tucked it tightly around him. No one would know there was anything under the pillow. She went out quietly, hoping that Storm's plan would work. She couldn't bear to think

of her friend having to leave suddenly
without warning.

Beth could hardly eat any lunch
because she was so worried about Storm.
She nibbled on a few mouthfuls of salad
and cauliflower and then asked if she
could leave the table.

"Are you feeling all right?" her aunt
asked.

"Fine, thanks. I'm just not very
hungry," Beth replied.

Martin glanced at Beth in concern and
seemed about to say something, but then
he changed his mind. He finished eating
and jumped up from the table.

"Why don't you and Storm come up
to the top field before lunch and see how
Dad and I are doing? We've cleared a lot

of it already. I'm going up there again now
with Ella. You could come with us, if you
like."

"I might. I'll . . . um . . . follow you
up there in a minute," Beth murmured
absently.

"Whatever," Martin muttered.

When he and Ella had left, Beth went
into the hall with a heavy heart. She was
dreading going upstairs to her bedroom.
Would Storm still be here or had her
friend already left forever?

Suddenly, a tiny fluffy black-and-white
figure came bounding down the stairs.
"Hello, Beth," Storm barked happily.

"Storm! You're still here!" Beth cried,
overjoyed, throwing her arms around him.

Storm yapped and licked her face, his
tail moving wildly. His midnight-blue eyes

were as bright as a moonlit sky and he seemed completely back to his usual self. "I cannot sense any strange dogs nearby, so they must have gone away. But if they return I might have to leave at once. We might not have time to say good-bye."

"I understand," Beth said, hardly taking this in. She just wanted to enjoy every single moment of the time they could spend together now.

She secretly hoped that Storm would stay with her forever, even though she knew he must someday return to help his injured mother and lead the Moon-claw wolf pack.

Beth decided to talk about something else. "Do you want to go watch Uncle Ollie giving Martin some plowing practice? It'll probably be really boring," she said, making a face.

Storm's cute face lit up, as it always did at any chance of a walk.

✦

Where's Uncle Ollie? Beth wondered as they walked toward the top field. She could see the red tractor and the plow mounted behind it, but only Martin and Ella stood beside it.

Storm was trotting beside her with his nose sniffing around on the ground.

Martin waved. "Hi! I didn't think you'd come," he shouted, sounding surprised and pleased.

Ella spotted Storm. She wagged her tail and trotted over, barking a greeting.

"I thought we might as well. Storm loves playing with Ella," Beth said, smiling at the dogs.

"Great. Now you can see what plowing's all about. Watch this," Martin called out. Leaping into Fergy's seat he started the engine and moved forward.

"Martin, don't! You're not supposed to be doing that!" Beth said worriedly, remembering her uncle's strict rules about Martin only driving under his supervision.

"I know what I'm doing!" Martin said huffily. "Anyway, I'll only plow a couple of furrows. Dad just went down to the barn for a can of lubricating oil—he'll never know. Unless you decide to tell him," he said, looking harshly at her.

"Thanks a lot. You should know by now that I don't tell!" Beth said indignantly.

Martin looked uncomfortable and then he gave a grin and nodded. Concentrating hard, he held the large steering wheel steady as the red tractor trundled slowly along, pulling the plow behind it. As he moved forward, the weedy ground was turned over and the soil curved away from the plow's metal moldboards in rich brown waves.

Despite herself, Beth was fascinated by watching the furrows form. Martin leaned over to watch the back wheels, making sure he kept driving in a perfectly straight line. The new brown furrow folded itself over and was laid neatly next to one previously made.

Beth realized that plowing took a lot of skill. "You're pretty good at this, aren't you?" she said, impressed.

Martin threw her a smile over his shoulder, obviously enjoying himself and pleased by her praise. "I'm not bad. But then I was taught by an expert. My dad!"

Suddenly Storm's head came up and his midnight-blue eyes flashed. Barking shrilly, he raced forward and began darting back and forth in front of Fergy's front wheels. "Stop! Stop!" he barked urgently.

"Martin! Watch out for Storm!" Beth cried.

"Why's he doing that? Make him stop!" Martin shouted.

Beth frowned. It wasn't like Storm

to do something so dangerous without
a good reason. But she was too worried
about him getting hurt to try and figure
out what that was.

"Come here, Storm! You'll get hurt!"
she shouted.

But Storm seemed determined.
Barking frantically, he ran even closer to
the tractor's ridged tires, snapping at them
and growling. One of the wheels passed
by him closely, missing him by a fraction.

As a stone flew out and hit him, Storm
gave a loud yelp.

"Martin! Look out!" Beth screamed,
thinking that Storm was about to be run
over.

Panicking, Martin jerked the tractor's
steering wheel to avoid the tiny puppy.
Fergy rolled to a halt. Martin turned off

the engine and jumped down.

"Look at that furrow. It's all messed up now. That stupid puppy made me mess up!" he fumed.

Storm stood by, panting heavily, his little sides heaving.

"Hang on! What's that? Look!" Beth interrupted, pointing at something half

buried in a weedy grass ditch that Martin
had been just about to plow over. As
Beth leaned over for a closer look, her
heart missed a beat. "I think it might be a
firecracker!"

Chapter
EIGHT

"Don't be crazy!" Martin said to Beth, walking over to take a look, but the moment he saw the metal object he frowned. "Oh! You're right. It does look like a firecracker. But it's probably been there for a while. Look, it's all shriveled and dented. I bet it's harmless."

"Storm didn't seem to think so," Beth reminded him.

Martin hesitated, chewing at his lip.

Beth guessed that he was worried
about getting into trouble for driving the
tractor. "Martin, this is an emergency. We
have to go and tell Uncle Ollie—now!"
she said.

"You're right," Martin decided. "Come
on!"

Beth didn't need to be told twice. She

bent down to pick up Storm and then turned on her heel and ran. Martin and Ella leaped after her and they all hurried back toward the farm as fast as they could.

Luckily Oliver was just coming out of the barn with an oil can. He raised his eyebrows when they raced straight up to him. "Where's the fire?" he joked, but his face grew serious as Martin and Beth began explaining.

"Good job, you two. You did the right thing. Firecrackers need expert handling. I'll call the emergency services and then alert the neighbors." He took his cell phone out of his jacket pocket and dialed. "Martin, will you go into the house and tell your mom, please?"

Martin nodded, his face now pale with worry.

Beth realized that her cousin had only just begun to grasp how serious this really was. Now that they were all a safe distance from the firecracker, she found herself shaking as it all sank in.

"Thank goodness you sensed the firecracker was there. You were very brave to get so close to the tractor and risk getting hurt," she whispered to Storm.

"I had to stop Martin somehow. We were too close for me to use my magic. Martin would have seen, but I could not risk anyone getting hurt," Storm woofed gently.

Beth and Storm stood in the yard with Martin, Ella, and her aunt as noisy police cars and fire engines arrived. Farm workers and their families began gathering, too.

Beth looked toward the top field, where the lights from half a dozen police cars were now flashing. She could see at least four fire engines. Bright-yellow hazard tape had been put up all around the site of the firecracker and across the field entrance.

"If it hadn't been for Storm, I'd have plowed right over that firecracker," Martin said. He bent down to pat Storm's head. "Thanks, boy. You might have just saved my life."

"You are welcome, Martin," Storm barked, wagging his tail, but of course only Beth could hear him speaking.

She beamed down at Storm, feeling very proud of her brave little friend.

Oliver came up and put a hand on his son's shoulder. "I should ground you for a week for driving Fergy when I specifically told you not to!" he said sternly.

"It wasn't my fault. Beth . . ." Martin started to make another excuse to get himself out of trouble, but then he seemed to think otherwise and hung his head. "Beth told me I shouldn't be driving Fergy by myself and she was right. I'm sorry, Dad."

"You always are," Oliver sighed. "But on this occasion it was lucky for all of us that things turned out this way. If I'd have been plowing and not you, I probably wouldn't have seen the firecracker until it was too late."

Martin looked subdued as he took this in and realized what it could have meant. He was silent for a moment, and then he brightened. "So I'm not in all that much trouble after all. Cool!"

"I give up!" His dad shook his head slowly and rolled his eyes.

"Look, someone in the field's waving a red flag," Beth noticed.

Just then Oliver's cell phone rang. He answered it and then spoke in a loud voice. "Listen up, everyone. There's going to be a controlled explosion in a few minutes. We shouldn't be alarmed. We're safe here."

Whump! A loud bang split the air.

Despite the early warning, Beth almost jumped out of her skin as the explosion echoed in her ears. An enormous spray of dark soil shot out in all directions and a thick dark smoke drifted upward.

"Yay! Way to go!" Martin shouted.

Everyone clapped and cheered. The danger was over.

"There'll be no more plowing in that field until the firemen have declared it safe. Do you hear me, Martin?" Oliver said.

"I wouldn't go up there now if you paid me," Martin said.

Beth could see that he meant it this time. Martin really seemed to be changing and Beth realized that she'd actually grown to like her grumpy cousin during her time at Tail End Farm!

"If you'd all like to come into the house I'll make coffee, and there's freshly made cake," Emily called out to everyone.

People began filing into the farmhouse. Martin called Ella and they followed them in. Beth was about to go in, too, when Storm suddenly barked with terror and ran toward the barn.

Beth heard a fierce growl behind her and looked around. She spotted two scary dogs running into the farmyard. As Beth saw their extra-long teeth and pale wolf-like eyes, she felt very fearful.

The dogs were under Shadow's spell. Storm's enemy had found him!

Without a second thought, Beth raced

into the barn ahead of the dogs. Somehow she knew where Storm would be. Darcy's pen!

She reached the pen at the back of the barn in time to see the tiny black-and-white puppy running into it. As the dogs pursuing Storm ran into the barn, there was a snort of rage and Darcy leaped right over the top bar of the pen and landed on the barn floor.

Braying threateningly, the billy goat ran straight at the fierce dogs with his head lowered. *Bang! Thud!* He butted them in the side, buying Storm precious time.

Suddenly there was a blinding gold flash and bright golden sparks rained down all around Beth and crackled onto the barn floor. Storm was no longer a tiny black-and-white puppy but instead stood before her as a young silver-gray wolf with glowing midnight-blue eyes. At his side was a huge she-wolf with a gentle face.

Beth knew the moment had come when Storm had to leave.

Storm lifted his magnificent head and looked at her with sad eyes. "Be of good heart, Beth. You have been a true friend," he growled in a deep velvety voice. He raised a large silver paw in farewell and then he and his mother faded and were gone.

There was a terrifying howl of rage behind Beth. The dogs' teeth and eyes instantly returned to normal, and they ran out of the barn.

Beth stood alone in the barn. A deep sadness welled up in her. She couldn't believe that Storm had left so suddenly. She was glad he was safe, but she was going to miss him terribly.

"I'll never forget you, Storm," she whispered, her throat closing with tears. She knew that she'd always treasure the time she had shared with the tiny magic puppy.

She heard steps behind her and

turned to see Darcy coming toward her.
He leaned forward to nuzzle her arm.
"You were really brave. Storm would be
so proud of you," she said, petting him
before leading him back to his pen. "The
sun's coming out. I think I'll ask Aunt Em
if you can go out in the field."

Darcy snickered delightedly as if he
understood.

"Talking to yourself again?" Martin

joked from behind her. "Are you coming into the farmhouse? I saved you a piece of cake."

As Beth turned to look at her cousin, she grinned. *Trust Martin to have the last word,* she thought, knowing somehow that Storm was watching them, his midnight-blue eyes glowing with approval.

Magic Puppy

Cloud Capers

SUE BENTLEY

To Ziggy—*four-squat and ugly-cute,*
but full of character.

Cloud Capers

SUE BENTLEY

Illustrated by Angela Swan

Grosset & Dunlap
An Imprint of Penguin Group (USA) LLC

Prologue

Storm, the young silver-gray wolf, barked with fear as a terrifying howl rose on the icy air and echoed over the dark mountain.

"Shadow!" Storm gasped.

The fierce lone wolf, who had killed Storm's father and three litter brothers and wounded his mother, was very close.

There was a dazzling bright flash and

a shower of gold sparks. Where Storm
had been standing there now crouched
a tiny Jack Russell puppy with soft
brown-and-white fur, a white tail, and
midnight-blue eyes.

Storm hoped this disguise would
protect him. He leaped toward a clump
of snow-covered rocks, his tiny puppy
heart beating fast. He needed to find
somewhere to hide—and quickly.

"In here, my son," growled a soft
velvety voice.

Storm plunged deeper into the
shadows and ran toward the she-wolf
who was slumped beneath a rocky shelf.
He recognized his mother immediately
and he licked his mother's muzzle.

Canista reached out a large silver
paw and drew the small puppy against

her thick warm fur. "I am glad to see that you arc safe and well. But you have returned at a dangerous time. Shadow wants to lead the Moon-claw pack, but the others will not follow him while you live."

Storm's midnight-blue eyes flashed with anger. "Then perhaps it is time for me to face him!"

"Bravely said," Canista growled softly. "But you are not yet strong enough to overcome him, and I am still too weak from Shadow's poisoned bite to help you. Use this puppy disguise. Go to the other world and hide. Return when your magic is stronger." As Canista finished speaking, she gasped with pain.

"Let me help you," Storm woofed, blowing out a cloud of golden sparkles.

They swirled around Canista's paw for a moment before sinking into her fur and disappearing.

Canista gave a sigh of relief as a tiny bit of her strength returned.

Suddenly, another fierce howl rang out, sounding much closer. Heavy paws scraped at the rocks and Storm could hear harsh breathing.

"Shadow has found your scent! Go now, Storm. Save yourself!" Canista urged.

Storm whimpered as dazzling gold sparks ignited in his short brown-and-white puppy fur and he felt the power surging through him. The gold glow around him grew brighter. And brighter . . .

Chapter
ONE

Jessica Tennant stood on the doorstep, clutching a bag of her favorite DVDs as she listened to her best friend's mom.

"I'm afraid Sheena's in bed with a bad cold and a sore throat. I was just about to call you. It's a shame that your weekend's ruined. You'll have to come and stay another time."

"Oh well, she can't help being sick,"

Jessica said, trying hard to hide her disappointment. "I'd better go." She held out the bag of DVDs. "She can borrow these. Maybe they'll cheer her up. Will you tell Sheena that I hope she feels better soon?"

Sheena's mom smiled. "That's really nice of you, Jessica. Sheena will probably call you in a couple of days."

As the front door closed, Jessica's shoulders slumped. She slowly walked back to her parents, who were waiting, parked outside in their van.

Mrs. Tennant looked at her daughter in surprise. "What's wrong? Why aren't you staying?" she asked.

Jessica shook her head. "Sheena's sick, so I can't stay. We were going to have a movie night and a midnight feast and everything. Now I don't know what to do," she said miserably.

"You'll just have to come with us to the Balloon Festival," her mom said.

Jessica made a face. She didn't want to go to the boring Balloon Festival with her parents. That's why she was going to stay with Sheena in the first place. "Can't

I stay with Gran and Gramps?"

"They're on vacation, remember?" Mrs. Tennant said.

"Well, what about Anjum?" Jessica said. "Oh, no . . . she's visiting her aunt. I know! I think Gemma's at home. We could ask—"

"Hang on, Jessica," her dad interrupted. "I'm afraid we don't have enough time to drive around to all your friends' houses on the off chance that you can stay with one of them. We have to get going. The rest of the High Flyers will already be on their way. Get in, please."

"But . . ." Jessica's face fell as she realized that she didn't have a choice. Sighing heavily, she climbed into the back and sat down. Leaning over, she threw her overnight bag under the seat.

"Cheer up, Jess," her mom said, turning around to smile as Mr. Tennant pulled the van away from the curb and headed out of town. "I don't like to see you with such a long face."

Jessica felt so fed up, she could feel her face getting longer and longer. It would sag right onto the floor at this rate.

"You might even have a good time. You used to think that hot-air ballooning with us was pretty exciting," her mom said.

"Yeah! That was when I was little and before I knew that I seriously hated heights and found out that you had to hang around for hours when the weather's not right for flying. Which is most of the time!" Jessica said bitterly.

Mrs. Tennant laughed. "You do exaggerate, Jessica Tennant! Anyway, the forecast's pretty good for this weekend."

Jessica wasn't excited by this news.

Mr. Tennant glanced at her in the rearview mirror. "You should be all right at Northampton. It's a really big festival. There'll be all kinds of stalls and displays and carnival rides to go on," he said cheerily.

"All by myself? Great," Jessica murmured through gritted teeth. She wished her mom and dad would stop trying to cheer her up. Nothing was going to make her feel better.

Crossing her arms, she slid down in her seat as they reached the highway and joined the endless stream of cars and

trucks. Time seemed to crawl, and the
next two hours felt more like two weeks.

When they eventually reached the
festival, Jessica saw tons of people putting
up stalls, erecting tents, and roping off
display areas. Mr. Tennant parked next to
a shiny motor home that was the size of

a single-decker bus. It made their van look very small.

"Look at that! It's even got its own satellite dish!" Jessica said, impressed despite herself.

"That's a Japanese model. They call those RVs. I bet you could live in that in the middle of a desert," her dad said.

"What's an RV?" Jessica asked.

"A recreational vehicle. I'd love one of those!" her dad said.

"We'd have to sell the house first," Mrs. Tennant commented. She went into the back of their van and began getting things out for lunch. "Could you go and get some water, please, Jessica?"

Jessica picked up a container and went trudging off across the parking lot. She really wished Sheena was here. She was missing her a lot.

As she walked past an empty tent at the side of the parking lot, Jessica spotted a girl coming toward her. The girl looked about twelve, two years older than Jessica, and she was wearing a cool T-shirt and jeans.

Jessica smiled. This looked like someone she might be able to make friends with. "Hi!" she said as the girl got closer. "Do you know where there's a water fountain?"

"Do I look like I'd know?" the girl snapped.

"I guess not," Jessica said, thinking that she seemed very grumpy. Maybe her parents had forced her to come with them, too. "Are you here with a balloon

club? I'm Jessica Tennant, by the way,"
she said, introducing herself.

"I'm Gayle Young. I'm with the
Cloud Racers. It's the best club ever,"
the girl said, tossing her long brown hair
over one shoulder.

"Dad says that about the High Flyers,
too," Jessica joked. "That's the club we
belong to."

"Huh! And I'm supposed to care?"
Gayle murmured, poking at the grass
with the toe of one expensive-looking
sneaker.

Jessica's smile wavered, but she kept
talking. "I saw some carnival rides and
stuff on the way in. Maybe we could
check them out together?" she suggested.

Gayle shrugged and wrinkled her
nose. "No thanks. I'm not into hanging

out with younger kids. I'm already stuck
looking after Mikey—he's my little
brother. I have to go now."

Jessica blushed as Gayle walked
past her, disappointed that she was so
unfriendly. "Well . . . er . . . good luck in
the balloon races tomorrow, anyway,"
she called.

Gayle didn't bother to look back.
"We don't need luck. The Cloud Racers
always win," she drawled.

Jessica watched the older girl walk
over to the huge RV and disappear
inside it. "Oh gr-eat! Some weekend
this is going to be!" she said to herself.

Jessica sighed and set off again to
look for water. Suddenly, there was a
flash of bright golden light and a crackle
of sparks from the tent next to her.

She frowned. Jessica had briefly
glanced inside as she passed and was sure
she hadn't seen anything in there. But,
she went to check anyway. As she had
thought, there was only an upside-down
cardboard box and some folded chairs
lying on the grass.

Then Jessica noticed the tiny brown-and-white Jack Russell puppy sitting on the box. Its fur seemed to be gleaming as if it had been sprinkled with gold dust.

"Hello. What are you doing in there all by yourself?" she said, walking slowly toward the puppy so she didn't scare it.

"I come from far away. Can you help me, please?" the puppy woofed.

Chapter
TWO

Jessica stared at the puppy in utter amazement. She must be more upset by Gayle's unfriendliness than she thought. She'd just imagined that the tiny puppy had spoken to her!

"I am Storm, of the Moon-claw pack. What is your name?" the puppy yapped, looking up at her with an intelligent expression.

"Whoa! You *can* talk!" Jessica gasped, dropping the plastic water jug and taking a step backward. "Are you part of an act or something?"

She quickly poked her head outside the tent's entrance to see if one of the festival entertainers was outside and playing a trick on her, but there was no one there. Jessica turned back to Storm. He was really cute with his soft brown-and-white fur, tiny pointed face, and the brightest midnight-blue eyes she had ever seen.

Storm sat there with his ears pricked, looking at her quizzically as if expecting an answer.

"I'm J-Jessica Tennant," Jessica found herself stuttering. "I'm . . . here with my mom and dad for . . . for the Balloon Festival."

She bent down and tried to make
herself seem smaller so as not to alarm
this amazing puppy. She still couldn't
believe this was happening to her and
she didn't want Storm to run away.

Storm dipped his head. "I am
pleased to meet you, Jessica."

"Um . . . me too." Jessica blinked as

she remembered something that Storm
had just said. "What's the Moon-claw
pack?"

"It is the wolf pack once led by my
father and my mother," Storm told her
proudly in a gruff little bark. "Shadow,
the evil lone wolf, killed my father and
three litter brothers and left my mother
injured. He wants to lead the pack, but
the others will not follow him while I
am alive."

"Hang on! Did you say *wolf*? But
you're a pu—"

"Please, stand back," Storm
ordered, jumping down from the box.

There was another blinding flash,
and the air fizzed with gold sparks
that fell harmlessly around Jessica and
sizzled on the grass.

"Oh!" Jessica rubbed her eyes and when she could see again she noticed that the tiny brown-and-white puppy was gone. In its place there stood a magnificent young silver-gray wolf with thick fur and huge velvety paws that seemed way too big for his body. Despite being young, the wolf had large sharp teeth and a thick neck-ruff that glittered with big golden sparkles.

Jessica looked at it warily. "Storm?"

"Yes, it is me, Jessica. Do not be afraid," Storm growled softly.

But before Jessica had time to get used to the majestic young wolf, there was a final gold flash and Storm reappeared as a tiny helpless brown-and-white puppy.

"Wow! You really are a wolf. That's an amazing disguise!" Jessica said.

Storm began to tremble all over, and his slender white tail drooped. "It will not save me if Shadow uses his magic to find me. I need to hide now. Can you help?" he asked.

Jessica's heart went out to him. She picked up the terrified puppy and petted his soft little head. "Of course I'll help you. You can live with m—"

She stopped as she remembered her parents' strict rules about pets. "Oh, I'm not going to be allowed to keep you. Back home, everyone's out all day and most weekends, too. Mom and Dad don't think it's fair to leave a pet by itself."

"I understand. Thank you for your kindness, Jessica. I will find someone else who can help me," Storm woofed politely, beginning to walk away toward the tent opening.

"Wait!" Jessica called out urgently. She wasn't ready to lose her new friend so easily. Before he'd arrived she'd been miserable. "There must be something I can do. Maybe I could hide you in our van. Except that it's really small and Mom and

Dad would probably find you." She had a
sudden thought. "Could you pretend to be
a toy dog? No, that wouldn't work either,
it would be too hard to stay really still and
not even blink."

Storm looked up at her with bright
midnight-blue eyes. "I can use my magic
so that only you will be able to see and
hear me."

"You can make yourself invisible?
Cool! Then I don't have to worry about
hiding you. You can sleep with me on the
sofa bed at the end of the van."

"I would like that very much. Thank
you, Jessica," Storm woofed. He leaned up
and she felt his wet nose brush her chin as
he began licking her face.

Jessica smiled down at the little
puppy. She felt her heart lighten as she

cuddled Storm's warm furry body. Her lonely boring weekend had just taken an unexpected turn!

Chapter
THREE

Jessica and Storm sat at the table under the awning, which her dad had put up outside the camper van. The other members of the High Flyers had arrived now and they were all having lunch together.

At first Jessica couldn't help worrying that someone was going to see Storm sitting on her lap, but when no one noticed him, she began to relax. After checking that she wasn't being watched, Jessica broke off pieces of her cheese sandwich and slipped them secretly to Storm.

The tiny puppy chomped them up eagerly and then jumped down onto

the grass. His tail wagged as he sniffed
the floor, licking up every last delicious
crumb. Jessica had to try really hard not to
giggle.

As soon as lunch was cleaned up,
Jessica's mom and dad and the other High
Flyers began unpacking the balloon and
equipment from a trailer.

Jessica had seen them do this hundreds
of times. She was about to suggest to
Storm that they go and take a walk, but he
seemed fascinated by what was happening.

"What is that big flat colored object
lying on the grass?" Storm woofed
curiously as he ran around with his
tongue hanging out. "Is it something to
play with?"

"No! That's the club's balloon. It's
made of a special light material but it's

collapsed right now so you can't see the shape. Hey! Don't go running around on it or you'll get a big surprise!" she called to him in a whisper as Storm looked like he was about to pounce onto the balloon. "Once they've got the burner ready, they'll light the jets and start filling the balloon with hot air."

Storm's tiny forehead wrinkled in a furry frown. "What happens then?"

"The balloon inflates and gets really big. It's tied down now, but if it wasn't it would float right up in the air. As high as the clouds."

Storm glanced upward, his big bright eyes sparkling in amazement. "Up there?" he woofed.

Jessica nodded. She pointed to the basket that was lying next to the balloon.

"See that? That's where Dad and the passengers stand when they go up in the balloon. You have to be a qualified pilot to be in charge. Dad's taken exams on flying and navigation and stuff. He's very experienced—he's won a lot of races!"

"But why do humans do this?" Storm wanted to know.

"It's a hobby. That's something you do for fun," Jessica explained.

Storm's midnight-blue eyes were as round as saucers—he couldn't believe that anyone would want to do such a strange thing. "Do *you* go up into the sky, Jessica?" he barked, looking very nervous.

"I used to, but I don't really like heights. My head feels really weird

and I feel sick and dizzy," Jessica said.
"I usually just watch from the ground
or go with Mom or someone else in
the support car to where the balloon
lands. Sometimes I stay in the van. But
now that you're here we can have fun
together."

Storm nodded, looking relieved, and
seemed to lose interest in the balloons.
"Does that mean lots of walks?" he
yapped, with a cute doggy grin.

"Definitely!" Jessica said, laughing.
"We can go for one now if you—"

There was a sudden loud hissing roar
as the burner ignited. A huge spurt of
bright-yellow flame shot out, and heated
air began flowing into the collapsed
balloon.

"Yikes!" Storm yelped, almost

jumping out of his fur. He ran sideways, and his fur rose in a ridge along his little back. "Fire!"

Jessica felt a strange warm tingling feeling flowing down her spine as big gold sparks ignited in the tiny puppy's brown-and-white fur and his ears and tail crackled with electricity. Storm raised a front paw and a fountain of gold glitter whooshed toward the burner.

There was a soft *phut!* and the gas jets went out.

Mr. Tennant looked puzzled. "That's weird. Maybe the jets need cleaning," he said, trying to light them again but without success.

"It's okay, Storm!" Jessica whispered quickly. "That's what's supposed to happen. Can you make the burner work again, please?"

Looking rather embarrassed, Storm sent more sparks shooting out of his paw. The jets lit immediately and a fresh burst of flame gushed out of them.

"That's it!" Mr. Tennant said.

Every last gold spark disappeared

from Storm's fur, but Jessica could see
that he was still frightened and shaky and
his little white tail was drooping.

Jessica quickly checked that everyone
was busy before pretending to bend down
and tie her sneaker. "Don't worry. There's
no danger. Dad knows a lot about health
and safety," she soothed, petting Storm's
soft little ears. "I'm sorry. I should have
explained that the burners make a scary
loud noise when you're not used to them."

Storm looked up at her trustingly and
began wagging his tail.

Jessica felt a surge of affection for
the brave little puppy who had stood his
ground and tried to help her, despite his
natural fear of fire.

"That's an ugly balloon! And the
basket's really small, isn't it?" said a

familiar voice behind Jessica.

Gayle! Jessica jumped quickly to her feet, her heart racing in case the older girl had seen her talking to Storm. But Gayle was watching the blue, purple, and white balloon rippling as it swelled to its full size.

"It's big enough for us. Dad has won

tons of trophies in it anyway," Jessica
replied.

Gayle curled her lip. "Sure he has,"
she said, making it obvious that she didn't
believe Jessica for a minute. Unexpectedly,
she smiled and her voice softened. "Why
don't you come and see our new balloon?
It's *so* cool."

Jessica thought about reminding Gayle
that she'd said she didn't want to hang out
with younger kids, but her curiosity got
the best of her. "Okay then. We might as
well . . . um . . . I mean—I might as well,"
Jessica corrected quickly. She would have
to be a lot more careful about keeping
Storm a secret.

Gayle gave her a weird look, but then
she smirked and turned on her heel.

As Jessica followed Gayle, Storm

trotted beside her. They wove through the other balloons and trailers and came to a big open space.

A vast black balloon in the shape of a snarling wolf's head was almost drifting upright. It hung there, connected to an enormous basket and tied to the ground. Jessica stared at it in astonishment. She thought the basket could hold about ten people. The noise from the twin burners was really loud.

A gust of wind blew the huge black balloon and it seemed to turn in Jessica's direction and grin down at her like a fierce monster.

Storm laid his ears back, shot behind Jessica's legs, and stood there trembling.

"What did I tell you? Isn't it amazing?" Gayle said triumphantly.

"It's not bad," Jessica said, determined not to sound too impressed. The Cloud Racers seemed to be a much bigger club than the High Flyers. She could see about twenty people around the enormous balloon.

Jessica noticed a small boy standing with them. He looked about six years old and wore a bright-red Spider-Man T-shirt.

Gayle saw where she was looking. "That's my brother, Mikey. He's not allowed to go up in the balloon because the rules say he's too short. That's why he follows me around when Mom and Dad are flying. He's really annoying," Gayle grumbled.

Mikey looked over at Jessica and gave a bright smile. He seemed really sweet.

*I don't think it's much fun for him either,
having to put up with a sister like Gayle,*
Jessica thought.

A blond woman stood next to Mikey.
She looked over and waved at Gayle and
Jessica. She was wearing a lot of bright
makeup, a floaty pink top, and high-
heeled sandals.

Gayle waved back. "That's my mom. Isn't she gorgeous? Just like a movie star."

"She's very pretty," Jessica commented, although she thought Mrs. Young looked a little too dressed up for ballooning. The other moms were wearing shorts, T-shirts, and sneakers.

"If you've seen enough, you can go back to your pathetic old balloon," Gayle said cheerfully. She walked across the grass toward her mom and little brother without looking back.

Jessica's jaw dropped. She'd just given Gayle another chance to be friends and had ended up being ditched—again!

"Is there anybody as annoying as Gayle Young?" she complained to Storm. "Come on. I'll just go and tell my parents that I'm going for a walk."

"I would like that," Storm woofed. He threw a final scared glance at the monstrous black wolf balloon before scampering after Jessica.

Chapter
FOUR

"It's a no-fly evening," Mr. Tennant said with a sigh a couple of hours later as he came into the van.

Jessica was sitting reading a magazine on the sofa bed with Storm curled up beside her. They watched a monster truck display and then a circus workshop. Now the tiny puppy's ears were twitching as he slept, and his tiny paws jerked as if he was running in his dreams.

As her dad came toward her, Jessica quickly shielded Storm with her magazine and scooped him into her lap.

"Wroof!" the tiny puppy yapped in shock, instantly awake and alert.

"Sorry to disturb you, but Dad's about to squish you," Jessica whispered as her dad plopped down next to her, exactly where Storm had just been lying.

"Look at this sunny weather. You'd never think the wind conditions were bad for flying, would you?" Mr. Tennant complained.

Jessica didn't have the heart to remind him that this happened a lot on ballooning weekends, which was another reason why she was sometimes bored. But things were different for her now that she had such a special friend. Storm!

She smiled to herself as she imagined the look on her dad's face if he knew that there was an invisible magic puppy a few inches away from him.

"Never mind, Dad. There's still the

nightglow," she said to him, patting his arm. "People always love seeing the balloons lit up by the burners in the dark while they're still roped to the ground."

He smiled. "Well, you've cheered up. I thought at one point you were going to be Miss Glum all weekend!"

"Da-ad! I wasn't that bad!" Jessica said.
She gave him a friendly shove.

He grinned. "Says who? If your face
had gotten any longer, you would have
tripped right over it!"

Jessica couldn't help laughing. Her dad
joined in.

After a few seconds, he wiped his eyes.
"Well, since there's no race this evening,
I'm going to start the barbecue. But first
I'm going to have a cold drink and relax."
He took a copy of Balloon Life magazine
out of a nearby cabinet.

With her dad nearby, Jessica couldn't
talk to Storm. She decided to take him for
a short walk. "I think I might take another
walk," she said to her dad.

Storm's ears pricked up immediately at
the possibility of a walk. He jumped down

with a soft *thud* and stood bright-eyed, wagging his tail hopefully.

Jessica smiled at him, feeling all light and happy. She realized that she wasn't missing Sheena that much anymore. She hoped her best friend wasn't feeling too sick.

Jessica and Storm set off in a roundabout way to avoid the tethered balloons and the noise of the gas burners, which Jessica knew still upset the little puppy.

They came to the biggest bouncy castle she had ever seen. It had dozens of towers and archways and things to climb on. There was even a giant slide. Kids were laughing and screaming as they bounced around having fun.

"Go on, you wimp. Just jump right

onto it. It's not going to bite you!" cried an impatient voice.

It was Gayle and she was with her little brother.

"Gayle's with Mikey. Let's go and see what's going on," Jessica said to Storm.

Storm woofed softly in agreement.

"I don't want to get on it. There are

too many big kids!" Gayle's little brother
wailed, backing away.

Jessica could see that Mikey was close
to tears but trying to hide it.

"You should have thought of
that before I paid for a ticket!" Gayle
complained. "It was out of my allowance
money, too, and I bet I won't get that
back. You're so annoying! Go on, Mikey.
Get up there!"

"No-oooo! Leave me alone," Mikey
sniffled.

Jessica felt herself getting angry. "Don't
be mean, Gayle. He doesn't have to go on
if he doesn't want to!" she said.

Gayle furiously turned around. "Who
asked you to stick your nose in? Mikey's
just chicken. *Cluck! Cluck!*" she mocked,
flapping her arms.

"I'm not chicken! I'm not!" Mikey burst into tears.

Jessica's temper snapped. She glared at Gayle. "You're just a mean bully!" she burst out.

Gayle narrowed her eyes. "Who are you calling names?"

Jessica gulped as the older girl took a step toward her. Gayle suddenly seemed very tall and tough.

Storm softly growled a warning and showed his sharp little teeth. Jessica felt another warm tingling sensation flowing down her spine.

Something very strange was about to happen.

Chapter
FIVE

As Jessica watched, big gold sparks
covered Storm's brown-and-white fur,
and his ears and tail fizzed with tiny
flashes of lightning. He raised a tiny front
paw, and a spray of shimmering glitter
shot out and whizzed around Gayle like
a mini-tornado.

Gayle froze as the magical sparkles
whirled faster and faster. A strange, blank

expression came over her face. Suddenly,
she turned around, ran forward, and
jumped straight up onto the bouncy
castle.

Gayle did two small bounces and then
on the third one she flew high into the
air before doing a triple somersault. As
soon as she landed she went straight up
again, somersaulted, and twisted into two
backflips.

The other kids stopped and watched her. They started clapping and cheering.

Mikey was no longer crying. His jaw dropped as he watched Gayle bouncing higher and higher, doing even more complicated jumps and twists.

"Aargh! What's happening?" Gayle cried, turning over and over, her arms spinning wildly and her legs working as if she was riding a bike.

"Hey! You! That's not allowed! Stop that at once!" the man in charge ordered, storming over.

"I can't! Help!" Gayle yelled, doing a handstand and another backflip. Suddenly, she did an extra-big bounce. She shot off the bouncy castle like a cork out of a bottle and landed on her feet a few feet away from Jessica. She stood there, swaying.

"I think I'm going to be sick," she groaned, her face looking green.

"Wow! That was awesome!" Mikey cried. "Watch me, Gayle!" He seemed to have lost all his nervousness as he jumped right onto the castle.

Gayle ignored him as she sank to the grass and sat there in a daze.

Jessica was trying hard not to laugh. "Storm!" she scolded gently.

Storm tucked his tail between his legs. "I am sorry. I think I used too much magic."

Jessica smiled at him. "Never mind. Maybe it'll teach Little Miss Bossy a lesson. And look at Mikey. He's really enjoying himself on the castle now! Come on, let's go for a walk."

Storm's midnight-blue eyes widened. "My favorite thing!"

Chapter
SIX

The delicious smell of barbecued sausages wafted toward Jessica as she and Storm walked back to the van about an hour later.

Her dad waved hello to her with a pair of tongs. He was wearing a new apron with a bright-green frog with big googly eyes on the front.

The other High Flyers were relaxing

nearby in camping chairs and talking about hot-air ballooning as usual. They greeted Jessica and smiled at her as she and Storm went across to her mom, who was sitting at the table making a salad.

"Hello, sweetie. Did you have a good time?" Mrs. Tennant asked.

"Yeah, we saw some people dressed as moving statues and there was a magician, but it's starting to get really busy now and Storm was almost getting stepped on—" Jessica broke off. She couldn't believe that she'd been so careless! But luckily her mom was busy cutting up tomatoes and didn't seem to have heard. "I ... um ... got tired of pushing through the crowds," she finished.

Her mom nodded. "I suppose people

are here for the nightglows and the
fireworks. Do you want one hot dog or
two?"

"Two please," Jessica said at once.
One for me and one for Storm, she thought,
hoping her mom wouldn't think she was
being greedy!

She took her plate and went to sit
on the grass while she ate. "Phew! That
was close. I'm so bad at keeping secrets. I
promise I'll get better!" she said to Storm.

Storm nodded as he chewed up his
hot dog.

After they all finished eating, Jessica
helped her mom clean up. The sky turned
violet with pink streaks as the sun set
and lights began turning on in the other
motor homes. Her dad and the other
High Flyers went to get the balloon ready

for the nightglow. "Should we go and watch?" Jessica's mom said, drying her hands.

"Okay. I'll follow you in a minute. I just want to get my bag. I think you'll be safer if you get inside it," she whispered to Storm.

Storm jumped right in with an eager little woof. As Jessica wandered across to the balloon display area, he settled down and poked out his head to look around.

The tethered balloons seemed dull and unimpressive against the evening sky, but at a signal all the burners were turned on. The balloons lit up, their beautiful colors shining green, gold, red, and blue, like glowing Chinese lanterns.

Storm yapped excitedly, forgetting to be nervous for a minute. "They are brighter than the Northern Lights that ripple across the sky in the long dark winter."

Jessica smiled, trying to imagine this wonderful sight. The other world where Storm lived as a young wolf must be very strange and wonderful.

Jessica caught sight of Gayle walking toward them. "Uh-oh, here comes trouble," she whispered.

As Gayle reached Jessica's mom and dad, she gave them a huge smile. "Hi. Isn't it a beautiful evening?" she called sweetly.

Jessica frowned. "Gayle is in a good mood. I wonder why."

"Hi! I came to find you. I thought you'd be watching the nightglow," Gayle said, smiling. She was twirling a necklace with a heart-shaped blue stone between her fingers. "Look what my dad just bought me. Do you like it?"

"It's really pretty," Jessica said.

Gayle smirked. "I know. Mom and Dad are really cool. They're always buying me presents. I bet you'd love a necklace like this."

Jessica shrugged. "Yeah, I guess. But I usually only get presents on my birthday or for special occasions."

"Poor you. What a shame that your mom and dad don't have a lot of money. Anyone can tell that by looking at your dirty old van," Gayle commented.

"I like our van and it's not dirty! It's only got a few scratches," Jessica exclaimed, starting to get annoyed again. She made a huge effort to calm down. It just wasn't worth getting all annoyed at Gayle's pathetic comments.

"That was really weird on the bouncy castle earlier, wasn't it?" Gayle said.

Jessica shrugged. "I guess so," she said.

Gayle was watching her closely. "I don't know what happened, but I bet you had something to do with it. I didn't think you had it in you," she said.

Jessica looked at Gayle in surprise and wondered whether she could actually be fun underneath it all.

"You just loved seeing me make a fool out of myself, didn't you?" Gayle commented.

"Well, it was pretty funny," Jessica said and then wished she hadn't. Gayle scowled, and the familiar mean look came over her face. She wasn't being friendly at all now—maybe she had just been pretending.

"You think you're so cool, don't you?" Gayle spat. "Well, no one makes fun of me and gets away with it! Just remember that!"

As Gayle stomped off, Jessica looked down at Storm with concern. "What do you think she means?"

Storm frowned at her from the bag. "It sounded as if she is going to try and get you back."

"Well, let her try!" Jessica said. "We'll be ready, won't we?"

She reached into her bag to pet Storm's smooth warm fur and didn't notice the concerned look on his tiny face.

Chapter
SEVEN

"There it is! That's our balloon!"
Jessica cried early the following
morning, pointing to a bead-sized blue
dot high in the sky.

Storm sat on Jessica's lap in the back
of the the High Flyers' support car.
Kim, who owned the car, was driving.
Jessica's mom was in the passenger seat
with a map and instruments on her lap.

They were carefully tracking the balloon, so that they would be in exactly the right spot to help with the landing.

"Grr-uff! Grr-uff!" Storm barked as he jumped up onto his hind legs and poked his nose out of the open window.

"Careful, Storm. Make sure you don't fall out," Jessica cautioned in a whisper.

It was 6:30 A.M. and conditions were

perfect for ballooning. The clear blue
sky overhead seemed filled with layers of
balloons of all shapes and sizes.

"Just look at that one!" Jessica said,
pointing to a giant rabbit that seemed to
be waving its paw. She could see a can
of soup and a big smiling head wearing
earphones, but her favorite was a crocodile
eating a packet of crackers.

"They are like giant creatures that
roar and spit fire and chase each other!"
Storm yapped. He still wasn't used to
the burners. A tiny growl rumbled in his
throat whenever the hissing roar of one of
them echoed on the still air.

"They're just dumb old sacks of
hot air. They won't hurt you," Jessica
soothed, petting his tense little body.

Storm gradually started to relax as

Kim headed out into the countryside
and drove through villages. By the time
they were getting close to a patchwork
of open fields, Jessica could see that the
High Flyers' balloon was beginning to
drift downward.

"They'll be coming down in the
fields somewhere over here," Mrs.
Tennant judged, pointing at a map with
her pencil. "We should go right at the
next crossroads."

"Got it," Kim said, concentrating
hard.

"This is the tricky part," Jessica
whispered to Storm. "Landing can be
dangerous because of power lines and
stuff. Sometimes the ground wind's too
strong and the basket tips over and the
balloon drags it along."

"That is not good. Someone could get hurt," Storm woofed worriedly.

"Yes, but Dad's a great pilot. You'll see. Here they come! Look!" Jessica waved to her dad, who was just a tiny figure in the basket at that moment.

Minutes later, Kim stopped the car and everyone got out. Jessica and Storm followed her mom and Kim across an unplowed field.

Suddenly, a huge black wolf balloon rose up from behind some tall trees and began descending rapidly.

Jessica ducked instinctively. "It's the Cloud Racers! They're going to land, too, but they're really close to our balloon!"

Storm gave a piercing whine of terror. He ran forward and hurtled across the field in a blind panic.

"Storm!" Jessica gasped. He must have thought that the monster balloon was about to attack him.

"Where did that puppy come from?" her mom cried.

Jessica realized that Storm was so scared that he must have forgotten to stay invisible. He wouldn't be able to use his magic to save himself without giving himself away!

Without a second thought, Jessica shot across the field after him. Her heart pounded as she ran, and her sneakers got covered in the muddy soil. The Cloud Racers' enormous black balloon seemed to blot out the entire sky, and the huge basket was barely five feet above her head. Glancing upward, Jessica caught a glimpse of horrified faces looking down at her.

Storm froze. He didn't seem to realize that he was right in the balloon's path. His midnight-blue eyes were like saucers, and his fur stood up along his back.

In desperation, Jessica threw herself forward. Her fingers brushed Storm's brown-and-white fur. Yes! She grabbed the tiny puppy and held him to her chest and then rolled over and over with him, as she'd been taught to do in gym class at school.

Just as she came to a stop beside the fence at the side of the field, she smashed her knee on a large half-buried stone. "Oh!" she gasped as a sharp pain took her breath away.

"Look out!" Jessica's mom and Kim were running across the field frantically waving their arms at the huge black balloon.

Jessica heard a shout from overhead. The powerful burners roared out, and the monster wolf balloon slowed. For an agonizingly long moment, it seemed to hang in the air and then it rose just high enough to sweep over her and Storm and skim the fence into the next field.

Jessica lay there, holding the shocked

puppy. Her entire leg seemed to be aching, and she couldn't move.

She saw her dad steering their balloon to a safe landing, thirty feet away across the field. Kim ran to catch the anchor rope, while Jessica's mom ran to where Jessica lay.

"Jessica! Are you all right?" Mrs. Tennant shouted anxiously.

"I'm okay, Mom. Just a little shaken up," Jessica cried.

Storm barked and reached up to lick Jessica's face. "Thank you for saving me. You were very brave."

"I wasn't really. I didn't think about it, but I just knew that I couldn't bear for anything to happen to you. Quick, you'd better become invisible again. Mom's almost here!" Jessica said, wincing.

"You have hurt yourself! I will make you better," Storm woofed.

Jessica felt the familiar tingling down her spine as Storm opened his mouth and huffed out a cloud of tiny gold sparks as fine as gold dust. The glittering mist swirled around Jessica's leg. The pain in her knee felt very hot for a second and then it turned ice cold and completely drained away like water gurgling down a drain.

"Thanks, Storm. I'm fine now," she said, quickly putting him on the ground and getting to her feet just as her mom reached her.

"You crazy girl! Whatever made you run after that puppy? You could have been really hurt!" Mrs. Tennant screamed, looking red-faced and shaky. "Where is the little puppy, anyway?"

"It . . . er . . . ran away through the h-hedge," Jessica mumbled hurriedly. "It must have been a stray. Anyway, I'm all right, Mom. Don't worry!"

"Jessica Tennant . . . ," her mom said darkly, looking as if she was about to make a very big scene.

Jessica swallowed and decided that

it might be best to change the subject. "Shouldn't we go and help Dad and the others?" she said quickly.

With Storm following her, she marched across the field to where Kim, her dad, and the others were dealing with the balloon.

Chapter
EIGHT

That evening, the weather was
perfect and the balloons were flying.
Jessica decided to stay behind with
Storm this time. She found a booth
selling cotton candy and then one selling
pet food and bought him a dog treat.

They went over toward the old
pavilion, where it wasn't so crowded, to
sit on the grass and eat.

"When do we go back to your home place, Jessica?" Storm woofed around a crunchy mouthful.

"Tomorrow. There's another race at six A.M. and then the award ceremony. After that we'll go home," she replied. "I can't wait for you to meet Sheena. She's going to love you!"

"I am sorry, Jessica, but you cannot tell anyone about me. Not even your friend." Storm's big dewy blue eyes were serious.

"Oh." Jessica felt disappointed that she couldn't even tell her best friend about Storm, but if that would keep him safe, she didn't mind too much.

Jessica ate the last of her cotton candy. She licked her fingers and stood up. "Finished?" she said to Storm.

Storm nodded. He leaped to his feet
and ran across the well-kept grass.

An old candy wrapper blew around,
and Storm's bright eyes sparked with
mischief as he pounced on it. Tossing his
head from side to side, he ran around
with the wrapper in his mouth.

Jessica smiled at his cute antics.
Sometimes it was hard to believe that

the adorable puppy was really a majestic
young silver-gray wolf who would one
day lead his pack.

Suddenly, Storm stopped. He stood
there quivering with concentration for
a few seconds and then gave a loud yelp
of terror and bolted straight into a flower
bed.

Jessica stiffened. But she couldn't
see what had frightened Storm. What
could be wrong? She raced over to the
flower bed and began searching beneath
a flowering bush.

"Storm? Where are you?" she called
anxiously.

At first she couldn't see any sign of
the little puppy, but then she spotted
him. He was tucked in a tight ball in a
space between two drooping branches.

"Is this a game or something? Oh, I get it. You're playing a trick on me!" she said, smiling, but then her face got serious when she saw that he was trembling all over.

"I saw a huge dog over by that tree. I think Shadow has used his magic to turn it into a wolf and send it after me!" Storm whined.

Jessica felt really scared. If Storm's enemy had found him, the tiny puppy was in terrible danger.

She glanced anxiously toward the tree and saw a woman with a big German shepherd dog on a leash. The dog saw her looking, and its tongue lolled in a friendly, doggy grin.

"Those dogs kind of look like wolves, but that one seems gentle,"

Jessica whispered uncertainly as the woman and her dog came closer. "How will I know if it's under a magic spell?"

"It will have fierce pale eyes and extra-long sharp teeth," Storm whined nervously.

Jessica looked at the German shepherd again. "It doesn't look like that. I think it's okay."

Storm crawled forward with his belly close to the ground and his tail between his legs. He peered through the drooping branches at the big dog, and Jessica saw him gradually relax.

"You are right. I am wrong this time. But if Shadow finds me, he *will* use his magic to hunt me down."

Jessica felt like she needed to comfort Storm. She bent down and picked Storm up as he crept out from under the bush. She could feel his little heart beating fast against her fingers. "I hope that horrible Shadow never finds you and then you can come home with me and stay forever!"

Storm looked up at her. "One day, I must return to my own world to help my mother and become leader of the

Moon-claw pack. Do you understand that, Jessica?" he yapped gently.

Jessica nodded, but she didn't want to think about that right now. "That was pretty scary. Let's go back to the van and spend some quiet time together," she said, changing the subject.

Storm reached up to lick her chin. "I would like that," he barked.

Jessica carried Storm to the parking lot. As they got closer to their van, they saw the door open and a girl peering out. After she quickly looked around, she climbed down and hurried away.

"That was Gayle. What's she doing in our van?" Jessica wondered.

Storm frowned. "I do not know."

"Maybe Mom came back to get something and Gayle was talking to her," Jessica said, knowing how Gayle was always careful to be on her best behavior around adults.

But when she went inside, she saw that the van was empty.

Storm stood with his head to one side.

"What is it?" Jessica asked him.

"Something is different . . ." Tiny gold sparks began twinkling in Storm's fur, and his wet brown nose began to glow like a gold nugget. With a triumphant woof he jumped up onto the back seat and began searching behind a cushion. A moment later, he emerged holding something in his mouth.

It was a gold necklace with a blue, heart-shaped stone.

Jessica recognized it. "That's Gayle's new necklace. She must have put it there. But why?"

"I think I know why!" Storm barked and then he pricked up his ears. "Someone is coming!" He picked up the necklace and dashed out of the open door with it in his mouth.

Puzzled, Jessica followed hard on his heels. "Storm? What's going on? Where are you go—" she started to ask and then stopped herself quickly as she saw Gayle and her mom standing there.

Mrs. Young was wearing a frilly blue dress and high heels. She had one arm around Gayle, who was dabbing at her eyes with a tissue.

"I want a word with you, young lady!" Mrs. Young said at once. "Gayle lost her new necklace and she thinks that you might know something about it!"

"Me?" Jessica said, almost speechless.

Gayle grinned slyly. "Don't try and look innocent," she sniffled. "I know you took it."

Jessica couldn't believe her ears. "I couldn't care less about your stupid necklace. I didn't take it!" she burst out.

"Huh! You would say that!" Gayle sneered. "I bet you've hidden it inside the van. Come on, Mom, let's go inside and look for it."

"Now wait just a minute!" said a deep voice behind them.

"Dad!" Jessica gave a cry of relief as her dad stepped forward.

"I heard all that," he said. "And I can assure you that my daughter's no thief. If

Jessica says she didn't take the necklace, I
believe her."

Mrs. Young gave him a charming
smile. Her teeth were very white against
her bright-pink lipstick. "In that case, you
won't mind if we come into your van and
have a look."

"I certainly do mind! Gayle probably
dropped that necklace somewhere. I
suggest you go and look for it, before you
come here making wild accusations," Mr.
Tennant said calmly.

"Well! If that's your attitude," Mrs. Young said indignantly, drawing herself up. "You haven't heard the last of this, I assure you. Come along, Gayle."

Gayle looked as if she was about to object, but she turned and hurried after her.

As Mrs. Young walked toward her motor home in her high heels, she suddenly stopped. "What's that glinting in the grass?" she said, bending down to pick something up. She turned to Gayle. "It's your necklace! You must have dropped it, just like Mr. Tennant said."

"But I don't get it! I put it under ... I mean ... I ... um ... didn't ...," Gayle stammered in confusion.

"You've made me look a complete

idiot!" Mrs. Young fumed, marching Gayle up the steps of the RV. "What have you been up to? And you'd better tell me the truth, or you'll be grounded!"

The door closed firmly and everything was silent. Jessica guessed that Gayle was getting a really severe lecture. She turned back to her dad. "Thanks for sticking up for me, Dad."

"No problem," he said, giving her shoulder a squeeze. "You haven't got a mean bone in your body, Jessica Tennant. But it was a good thing we got back here in time."

Just as her dad went into the van, Storm came out from underneath the van and ran up to Jessica.

"Thanks, Storm. That was a great

idea to drop Gayle's necklace over by the RV. It really turned the tables on her!"

"You are welcome, Jessica. I do not think she will be making any more trouble," he yapped happily.

Chapter
NINE

Jessica woke up early on Sunday morning. Pale lemon sunlight was just pushing through the crack in the van's curtains.

Storm was lying next to her. He wagged his little tail as she petted him, and snuggled back under the warm blanket with a contented sigh.

Even though it was early, Jessica was

wide awake. Leaving Storm lying there, she carefully climbed over him and dressed in shorts and a T-shirt. After boiling some water for tea, she brought her mom and dad a cup of tea in bed.

"Thanks, sweetie. You're an early bird today!" Mr. Tennant sat up looking sleepy-eyed and with his hair all messy. "You're not making breakfast, too, are you?" he asked hopefully.

Jessica took the hint. "Eggs on toast?"

By the time they were cleaning up the
cups and plates, the other High Flyers had
arrived. Kim had bad news.

"It's going to be another no-fly
day," she announced. "So the winning
times have been worked out from Friday's
and Saturday's flights. We're in second place.
The Cloud Racers are first."

Mr. Tennant nodded. "Ah well, that's
how it goes," he said good-naturedly. "It's
a shame we won't get a chance for another
flight. But there'll still be a balloon tether
before we pack up for good."

"That's when the balloons are roped
to the ground and just hover a few inches
in the air. No balloon monsters high
in the sky to scare you today," Jessica
explained in a whisper to Storm.

Outside in the enclosure, cars and
trailers had parked and the grass was
already covered with acres of brightly
colored nylon. Jessica could see that the
Cloud Racers' basket lay on its side. The
burners were going, and the huge black
wolf face was almost fully inflated.

She and Storm were standing with
her mom and dad when Gayle's parents
approached them. Mrs. Young was holding
Mikey's hand.

"Have you seen Gayle?" Mr. Young
asked Jessica.

Jessica shook her head, puzzled. "No, I
haven't seen her since yesterday."

She noticed that Mrs. Young looked
different and then realized why. Gayle's
mom was in jeans and a crumpled
T-shirt and she wasn't wearing make-up.

Her eyes looked puffy as if she'd been
crying.

"Is something wrong?" Mrs. Tennant
asked her gently.

"It's Gayle. She's missing," Mrs. Young
said with a shaky voice. "We had a bit
of a fight about this necklace business.
I thought at first that she'd gone off
somewhere sulking by herself—she's done
it before. But it's been over an hour now

and I'm starting to get really worried."

"I'll help you look for her," Jessica
offered at once.

"That's very nice of you, especially
after the way Gayle behaved," Mr.
Young said.

"Anyone can make a mistake,"
Jessica said generously.

"Let's all spread out and look
around," Mr. Tennant suggested.

"Good idea. I'll look over here,"
Jessica said, walking off with Storm.
She waited until her mom and dad had
gone in opposite directions and then
turned to Storm. "Do you think you
can pick up Gayle's scent?" she asked.

"I will try," Storm woofed.

Scampering over to the Youngs' RV,
he began sniffing around in the grass.

Jessica followed him and watched
as he worked his way back and forth.
Moments later, his head came up. "This
way," he yapped triumphantly.

Jessica ran after him as he headed
toward the line of tethered balloons.
The Cloud Racers' huge black
balloon and basket were floating a
few inches above the ground. Two of
the club members were standing with
their backs to the balloon.

Jessica caught a sudden movement
from the corner of her eye. A slim
figure suddenly dashed out from behind
a van and quick as a flash scrambled
unseen into the huge basket.

"It's Gayle!" Jessica gasped, rushing
forward with Storm at her heels.

As she ran up to the balloon, she

saw Gayle lean over, unhook a rope,
and drop it to the ground. The basket
wobbled and tipped at a crazy angle.

The two club members turned.
They realized what was happening and
quickly grabbed a rope each, but the
balloon began to rise slowly as Gayle
unhooked another rope and threw it
down.

"Gayle, don't!" Jessica cried.

Gayle glared at her. "What do you
care? You don't like me. Everyone hates
me!" The balloon rose up higher, almost
free.

"I don't hate you, and your mom
and dad are really worried about you.
Just stay still and let the team get you
down," Jessica pleaded.

Gayle bit her lip and looked as

if she might be starting to believe Jessica.

"Gayle! What on earth do you think you're doing? Get down from there!" Mr. Young ordered as he, his wife, and Mikey ran toward the balloon.

Then everything happened at once.

The club members, already on tiptoe and trying to hold down the balloon, were lifted off their feet. They dropped to the ground as the black balloon rose into the air, trailing ropes and taking Gayle up with it.

Jessica saw the balloon ripple as if it was caught in a side wind. It lurched sideways, and the wolf face seemed to leer as it started to collapse.

Gayle screamed and clung on to the basket.

Jessica gasped in horror. The whole thing was going to come crashing down!

Chapter
TEN

Time seemed to stand still.

Huge gold sparks bloomed in Storm's brown-and-white fur and his ears fizzed with power. He shot into the air, with a comet's tail of sparkles behind him, and landed in the basket next to Gayle.

Jessica saw a burst of flame shoot out of the gas jets. Hot air flowed into the balloon, which swelled out and

straightened itself. At the same time a
gush of gold sparkles erupted in the
basket, and ropes snaked downward
toward the ground.

Eager hands reached for them, and
they were quickly secured. People ran
to help, and the balloon was drawn
downward until the basket rested on the
grass.

Jessica saw Storm leap out and streak
toward her.

Gayle's dad leaped into the basket
and gave his daughter a huge hug. "Are
you all right, sweetie? I was terrified
that you were going to be hurt. Thank
goodness that you had the sense to work
the burner and throw down those extra
ropes."

Gayle was white-faced. She didn't

seem to know whether to laugh or cry. "Burner? But I . . . ," she stammered shakily.

But her dad wasn't listening. He helped Gayle climb out of the basket and one of the club members reached forward to help her. Everyone cheered and clapped.

Gayle hung her head and chewed at her lip. "Thanks, everyone. I—I didn't mean for that to happen. I'm glad that no one got hurt because of me."

Jessica could see that, for once, Gayle really meant it.

She looked down at Storm, who stood beside her. Every last spark had faded from his fur. She wished she could cuddle him, but there were too many people around for her to pick him up.

"That was incredibly brave of you to light the burner, Storm. I know how fire scares you," she whispered.

"I am just glad that Gayle is safe. But I do not think I will ever grow to like hot-air balloons," he barked.

Jessica noticed Gayle looking at her in a very strange way. She realized that the older girl had heard her whispering to Storm!

Gayle smiled knowingly and then she shrugged. "Weird things keep happening when you're around, Jessica. I'd love to know what's been going on, but I guess I never will. Keep your secrets. It's fine by me. And thanks for trying to help me. I'm sorry for being such a pain. Can we start all over again and try to be friends?"

"I'd like that," Jessica replied, pleased.

"Cool! Why don't you come over
to our RV? You haven't seen inside yet,
right? It's got a huge shower room and
a TV and everything."

Jessica smiled. Gayle would never
change, but at least she was trying to be
a lot nicer now. "Okay, thanks. I'd love
to see inside it," she said.

Gayle beamed at her. She reached for
Mikey's hand before walking off with her
parents. "See you in a minute, Jessica."

With the excitement over, people
began dispersing. Suddenly, Storm
whimpered and began trembling all over.
He took off like a rocket and headed
toward a clump of thick bushes a few feet
away.

"I'll . . . I'll be right back!" Jessica
said to her mom. She hurtled after the

terrified puppy, a terrible suspicion rising
in her mind.

She spotted three dogs running toward
the bushes from the opposite direction.
They had fierce pale eyes and extra-long
sharp teeth. Shadow had put a spell on
them. They were here for Storm.

As Jessica pushed her way into the
center of the bushes there was a dazzling
flash of bright gold light.

Storm stood there; he was no longer
a tiny brown-and-white Jack Russell
puppy. He was a majestic young wolf with
thick silver-gray fur. A thousand tiny gold
diamonds sparkled in his neck-ruff. Beside
him stood an older she-wolf with a gentle
expression on her face.

At that moment, Jessica knew that
Storm must leave her. Her throat clenched
with sadness, but she forced herself to be
brave. "Save yourself, Storm!" she cried.

"Be of good heart, Jessica. You have
been a loyal friend," Storm said in a deep
velvety growl.

There was a final burst of intense
gold light, and a silent explosion of sparks
crackled down around Jessica. Storm and
his mother faded and were gone.

There was a growl of rage as the fierce

dogs burst through the bushes. Seeing that Storm had disappeared, their eyes and teeth instantly returned to normal and they fled.

Jessica felt stunned. It had all happened so fast. Her heart was aching, but at least she'd had a chance to say good-bye. Storm was safe, and she hoped that one day he would be able to stay in his own world and lead the Moon-claw pack.

Tears pricked her eyes as she slowly began walking back toward the parking lot. Jessica knew she would never forget her wonderful adventure with Storm.

She thought of Sheena and hoped she was feeling better. Jessica decided to buy her a cuddly toy to cheer her up. Then she smiled as she saw Gayle waiting for her. Perhaps she'd get Gayle one, too. A cute toy puppy for both of them.

After all, she thought, *everyone should have their own magic puppy.*

About the
AUTHOR

Sue Bentley's books for children often
include animals, fairies, and wildlife. She
lives in Northampton, England, and enjoys
reading, going to the movies, relaxing
by her garden pond, and watching the
birds feeding their babies on the lawn.
At school she was always getting yelled
at for daydreaming or staring out of the
window—but she now realizes that she
was storing up ideas for when she became
a writer. She has met and owned many
cats and dogs, and each one has brought a
special kind of magic to her life.

Don't miss these Magic Puppy books!

Don't miss these Magic Kitten books!

Don't miss these Magic Bunny books!

#1 Chocolate Wishes

#2 Vacation Dreams

#3 A Splash of Magic

#4 Classroom Capers

#5 Dancing Days

Don't miss these Magic Ponies books!